THE GUILTY ONE

KIERSTEN MODGLIN

KIERSTEN
MODGLIN
Love Lies, Alibis

Cover Design by Kiersten Modglin
Copy Editing by Three Owls Editing
Proofreading by My Brother's Editor
Formatting & Graphic Design by Kiersten Modglin
Author Photograph © Lisa Christianson

First Print and Electronic Edition: 2024
kierstenmodglinauthor.com

To the truth tellers and fighters for justice—
the ones who stand up to friends in kindness
as quickly as enemies

"Silence of the good is the weapon of the wicked."

VERA BITTER

CHAPTER ONE

CELINE

When the call comes in, I nearly ignore it. I assume it is probably a scammer, someone trying to tell me about my car's extended warranty expiring or to sell me something I don't need for a price I can't afford.

I'm not sure what causes me to change my mind. Perhaps it's the fact that the area code is local, though that doesn't always mean it is safe. Maybe it is something deeper than that, a sort of gut feeling that something is terribly wrong. The only way I can think of to describe it is that it is the sort of knowing many people talk about but few have ever experienced. At least, I've never experienced anything like it.

In the end, I do answer my phone, and when I do, I hear a voice and a phrase I'm certain I'll forever have nightmares about.

"Is this Celine Thompson?"

I swallow, my throat suddenly too dry. I step farther

into the hallway, pressing a finger to my ear to drown out the sounds of the customers and machines in the background. There's something ironic and cruel about the fact that my world is falling apart at the exact moment someone is ordering a mocha breve with oat milk and extra caramel.

"Yes, it is."

"My name is Officer Simone with the Oakton County Police Department. I'm calling about a Tatum Thompson. He has you listed as an emergency contact in his phone."

Tate. A pang of sadness shoots through my heart, and all I want to do is see him right now. My chest aches suddenly with worry. *Something must be wrong.* "That's my husband."

The woman on the phone draws in a deep breath, keeping her voice steady and calm. "Ma'am, I'm so sorry to have to tell you this, but this afternoon your husband was involved in an accident in which he sustained injuries he was unable to survive." I have absolutely no idea what she says next, only that she keeps talking for what feels like an eternity while my brain sputters and gasps and tries to process everything I'm being told.

Minutes, hours, or days later, when the phone call ends, I know what she has told me. The stuff that matters, anyway.

My husband has been involved in a car crash.

He is dead.

I need to go to the police station to identify the body.

Back behind the counter, I find my supervisor and pull her aside in a sort of catatonic state. Margie is the kind of person who lives and breathes our job. She has worked for The Bold Bean for as long as it's been open, and I'm still not sure it won't be forced to close the day she retires.

She isn't an unkind person, she's just the type of boss who finds it hard to believe anyone could possibly have a life outside of the coffee shop that pays our bills.

I don't remember much of the conversation between us, just that I rush to tell her, between my tears, that something has happened to Tate and I need to leave, and that she will have to find someone to come in to cover the rest of my shift. I don't wait for her to grant permission—the simple act of telling her instead of running out the door immediately feels like more than enough, so with that taken care of, I hurry to my car as fast as my legs will carry me.

In the small parking lot, I put the police station's address into my GPS, my mind a blurry mess of terror, confusion, and heartbreak as I drive across town and soon find myself walking into the building where my life will forever change.

Once inside, I'm directed to a room where a woman with dark hair and fair skin who looks not much older than I am sits down across from me and introduces herself as Officer Simone. It's the same voice I spoke to on the phone, and somehow, each time she speaks, it's a shot to the heart.

"When will I get to see him?" I ask, wringing my hands together in my lap.

She places her hands on top of the table, smoothing them out calmly. "The way this works is I'm going to show you a few photographs the medical examiner took of your husband's body after the crash." She picks up a folder from the seat beside her, laying it down on the table. "These photographs will help—"

"Photographs?" That doesn't make any sense. *Why isn't she taking me to see him? I need to see him. Not photographs. His body. I need to see his body.* "What are you talking about? Why can't I see his body?"

She pauses, her eyes searching mine with a sort of frustrated compassion. Her next sentence explains why. "I know television shows would have you believe that's how this happens, but in reality, this situation is about minimizing trauma to the family, not creating dramatic moments, Mrs. Thompson. Your husband sustained serious bodily injuries in the crash. Of course, his body is in the morgue, and we can arrange for you to see it, but please know that I would strongly advise against that. This process is designed to prepare you for what you'll see, to minimize the trauma of what you'll have to see, and to make sure you feel safe and supported during this time. None of this is easy, we just want to make it as comfortable as possible. I also have the contact information for an excellent grief counselor that I'm happy to provide you with."

I swallow. Of course this isn't like the crime shows Tate and I watch together. Just the thought of him, of those memories, sends another wave of pain through me. I'll never get to see his face when he correctly guesses the murderer before it's revealed again, never get to hear him bragging as he catches a blooper.

Everything about my life is about to change into something unrecognizable.

Clearing her throat and sitting straighter in her seat, she goes on, "Now, whenever you're ready, just so you know what to expect from these photographs, your husband's face has several severe lacerations across both his right and left brows, down his forehead, and across his temple. The skin on the right side of his face is, for the most part, missing due to his injuries. You will notice that his mouth is concave due to the accident causing him to lose several of his teeth."

I think I'm going to be sick. Or pass out. Every breath I take is so loud in my ears.

"He was cleaned up to the best of our abilities before the photos were taken, but I want to prepare you for what you're going to see. There is also a photograph of a tattoo on his right shoulder, a birthmark on his hip, and a photograph of the wedding ring he was wearing. Your husband's injuries were severe, and though our team made their best effort to keep the photographs tasteful, you will likely find the photo of his face especially gruesome, Mrs. Thompson. As I said, this process is designed to minimize trauma for people in your position, but I still want you to know that this will likely be traumatic for you, and that's completely understandable and to be expected. Please take your time looking at these photos. No one here is going to rush you, okay?" She slides the folder toward me cautiously, lifting her hand. "Take all the time you need."

I replace her hand with mine, pulling the brown folder the rest of the way across the table and glancing down. The second I open the folder, I know everything is going to change. It has to. Once I look into his face—the face I kissed just this morning before he left for work—and know he is gone, all of this will be real.

No more pretending.

The officer sits quietly, waiting patiently just like she promised she would while I stare down at the brown folder, my heart pounding in my chest. I don't want to open it. I want to pretend like none of this is happening. I want to go back to this morning and pretend, for just a few more minutes, that life is normal.

But it isn't, and it will never be the old version of normal again.

All I have to do is open the folder and prove it. And so, with a deep breath and tense muscles, I do. I flip the folder open, holding my breath, and stare down at the photograph on top.

My breath catches in my throat. It's the lion tattoo on his shoulder that I've stared at each morning while he brushes his teeth, or every time we've showered together. The one I've rubbed sunscreen over during summer vacations to the lake or the beach.

Tears line my eyes at once, blurring my vision, and I move the photo just in time to prevent it from getting wet as the tears cascade off my cheeks. I'm already nodding, already confirming, when I lift the photo to see the next one, and it's the one she warned me about. Bile rises in my throat as I take in the remaining features of his face—the ones that weren't destroyed by the accident.

Except...it *isn't* his face.

I blink, drying my eyes, and lift the photograph closer to my face, trying to understand. It doesn't make sense.

Seeming to realize that something is wrong, the officer leans forward. "Ma'am? Is everything alright?"

"It's...it's not him," I say, my voice soft and trembling as though I'm afraid if I speak the words too loudly, the universe might hear me and correct its mistake.

"Ma'am?" she asks again, her voice rising with tension. "What do you mean?"

Shaking my head, with new, fresh, more persistent tears filling my eyes, I force myself to look more closely. He has dark hair like Tate, pale skin, and with the bruises and wounds, it's possible for him to pass as my husband to an outsider perhaps, but not to me.

I know Tate's features. I've spent years of my life studying them, being mesmerized by them. Falling in love with them. These features are different. This man is different.

I pass the photograph back to her. "The tattoo…it's his, but…this isn't my husband." I jab my finger into the photograph, into the face I don't recognize. "I have no idea who this is."

CHAPTER TWO

CELINE

The officer just stares at me as if I've grown a second head. As if there could be a chance I might not recognize the man I married, might just be mistaken when I say the face they're showing me isn't his.

"This man isn't your husband?" She points toward the photograph again, sliding it closer to me.

I shake my head, sniffling as more tears come. Tears of relief this time. Of confusion. "No. I...I've never seen this man."

"With injuries of this extent, it would be understandable if you had a hard time recognizing him."

"It's not that. I know my husband's face. His nose is different. His eyes are smaller. This isn't my husband, I'm positive."

"He was driving your husband's car," she says, turning the photograph around and lifting it so she can stare at the man's face. "He was carrying his phone and

ID." She's talking to herself now as she stands. "You said…you said the tattoo *is* a match, though?"

Suddenly, I realize we're thinking the same thing: did the face photographs get mixed up?

How many car crash victims did they have today? How many bodies are there to identify?

I picture a lineup of devastated wives, filing into this room one after the next.

Looking down, I realize there are still two other photographs she gave me to look at. A ring placed next to a hand—a hand that's supposed to be his—and a birthmark. With trembling fingers, I examine both photographs before shaking my head. My lungs release air as if it's sadness and I can't get it out of me quickly enough.

"It's not him," I tell her, pushing the photographs away. "He doesn't have a birthmark on his hip, and his ring is custom—inlaid with wood from a bourbon barrel with a guitar string on top. I got it for him on our anniversary a few years ago. Plus his hands have burn scars on them from an accident years ago. They're light but noticeable up close. Especially along his thumb. The hands in the photograph don't have scars."

Her face is serious as she turns away, preparing to leave the room, then turns back one last time. "You're absolutely sure."

I close the folder and slide it back to her, keeping my voice as steady as I can. "It's not Tate."

She gathers the photos, hurriedly shoving them

back into the folder. "I'll be right back, Mrs. Thompson. Please wait here."

I swallow and look down, gathering my hands in my lap as I try to understand what might be happening. The tattoo was his, the car, the phone, and wallet were his, but the ring, hands, face, and birthmark were not.

Does this mean there's a chance he's alive?

My throat clenches, and I want to call him, to hear his voice, but the police have his phone, so I'd simply be calling them. Still, I have to try.

I pull out my phone and find his name in my call log, clicking on it. I press the phone to my ear, my heart in my throat as I listen to it ringing.

Pick up.

Pick up.

Pick up.

Please pick up and tell me this has all been a misunderstanding. Laugh and ask what in the world I'm talking about. Tell me I should've called you before I rushed to the police station. Tell me you're coming for me right now. Come and get me and—

"You've reached Tate Thompson with Morris Realty. I'm sorry I couldn't get to the phone right now, but if you'll leave your name and number, I'll call you back soon. Thanks."

With tears in my eyes, I end the call. It was a long shot. I knew that, but it was a bit of hope I was still clinging to.

Where are you, Tate?

My chest feels hollow as I sit and wait, wanting nothing more than to get out of here and go look for my husband. When Officer Simone returns with two more officers in tow, I have a feeling it's going to be a long time before I can do that.

The officers take their seats across from me, one pulling a chair from my side around to hers.

"Mrs. Thompson," Officer Simone says, "these are my colleagues, Officer Chatham and Detective Monroe. We want to ask you a few other questions surrounding this investigation."

It sounds so formal now. It went from a car crash— a terrible accident—to an investigation.

I nod, leaning forward. "Okay. Sure."

"Officer Simone says you can't confirm that the man who was driving your husband's car was your husband," Officer Chatham says. She's older than Officer Simone, I'd guess, with thin wrinkles around her eyes and mouth. She has a kind but firm smile that tells me she means business.

Next to her, Detective Monroe, a Black man with a buzz cut, stares at me without saying a word.

"I can confirm that it's *not* him," I tell them. "It's not."

The detective places the folder back on the table and opens it once again, spreading out the photographs so I can see each of them in a row. "This man," he says, pressing his finger into the photograph next to the man's temple, "is not your husband? He isn't Tatum Thompson?"

"No," I tell them. "I've never seen this man in my life. It's not my husband." *Why do I get the feeling they don't believe me?*

"How do you think a stranger would have come to be driving your husband's car, ma'am?" Officer Simone asks.

"I have no idea," I tell her. "But...you said you have his driver's license. Surely you can tell the photo isn't of this man." Even as I say it, I know it's a long shot because this man does bear a passing resemblance to my husband. They have similar square head shapes, dark hair and brows. They are around the same height and weight. Still, it isn't him. I know it isn't. "Maybe he robbed him. Maybe he took his wallet and phone and car."

The officers exchange glances. "Are you able to place a few phone calls for us, ma'am? To anyone you believe might know your husband's whereabouts? His family, his friends, coworkers..."

"Yes, of course." I should've already thought of that. *Why isn't my brain working?* I feel as if I'm drowning. I pull out my phone, staring down at the photo of the two of us and our boys. My heart plummets when I see the time. "Oh my god, my kids. I'm sorry. I need to..." I stand up, not finishing the sentence as I search for my mom's name in my call log.

After the fourth ring, I'm about to end the call when she finally picks up. "Hello?"

"Mom…" I sob. "I need you to pick up the boys from school."

"What? What's going on? What's wrong?"

"I'll explain later," I promise, though I have no clue how I'm going to explain any of this to anyone, myself included. "Can you get them for me?"

"Of course, babe. I'm on my way home from the store anyway, so I'll swing by the school right now and get them. Is everything okay?"

"I don't know," I answer honestly. "I'll come by your house as soon as I can."

"You're scaring me," she says softly.

"I know. I'm sorry. I just…I have to go, okay? Give them a kiss for me."

"I will."

"Oh, hey, before I let you go…you haven't heard from Tate, have you?"

She hesitates. "Heard from Tate? What do you mean? Today? Was I supposed to?"

"No, it's fine. I just…I'll see you soon, okay? I love you."

"You too, sweetheart. See you soon."

I turn back to the desk and begin scrolling through my contacts. I find my mother-in-law's name first and click on it. Unlike my mother, she answers quickly.

"Hey, honey! What are you up to? I was just

thinking about you earlier because I found this recipe for a lemon—"

"Daph, I'm sorry, I don't have time to chat. I was just wondering if you've talked to Tate today?"

"Oh. Talked to Tate? Today?" She hums. "No, it's been a few days since we spoke, I suppose. Why?"

"Do you know if Lane has?"

"I'm not sure. Well, actually, he's right here. Let me ask him. Is everything alright?" I can hear her speaking to my father-in-law in the background, her voice muffled.

I have no idea what I'm supposed to tell them, if anything.

"Neither of us have spoken to him today, honey. Is something wrong?"

"I'm..." My voice cracks, and I do my best to collect myself. "There was a car accident, and...we can't find him."

She's quiet, then my father-in-law comes on the line. "A car accident?" he demands. "What are you talking about? He was involved?"

"It was his car, but someone else was in it. I'm just trying to track him down."

"Where are you?" he demands.

"The police station."

"The police station?" His voice rises an octave. "What for? Do you need us to come down there? Are you alright? Are you hurt?"

"No. No. I'm okay. I'm fine. It's just...the person

involved, the man in Tate's car he…he's dead, Lane. They thought it was Tate."

Now we're all crying, trying to talk over each other as we make sense of it.

"What do you mean—"

"Have you called him—"

"I just saw him a few days ago—"

"Yes, he was okay this morning—"

"Where are the boys?"

"We're coming down there—"

"No, just…just meet me at the house, will you? I'm going to call his boss and see if he's been in the office today or where he's supposed to be. I'll let you know when we find him."

My mother-in-law's voice is soft when she speaks. "Where are the boys?"

"My mom is picking them up. I'll be home soon, okay?"

"We'll go to her house then," she says. "We should be together. All of us. Until we sort this out."

I nod, though she can't see me. "Okay."

"We'll see you soon," Lane says.

I end the call and search for Tate's office number. His boss is rarely in, but at least I'll be able to get a hold of someone who can help me track him down.

"Morris Realty, Dustin speaking, how can we help you find a home today?" comes the chipper voice through the line over the distinct sound of typing.

"Dustin, this is Celine Thompson, Tate's wife. I was

wondering if he was in the office today or if you might know where he's supposed to be right now."

"Heya, Celine," he sings. "Long time, no see. Let me just check and see if he's in. I don't think I've seen him, but sometimes he likes to sneak in on me." The typing continues, then stops abruptly. "Oh shoot, that's right."

"What's wrong?" My blood chills in my veins.

"Well, hang on just a second for me. Hmm…yeah, let me just see something." He pauses, then sucks in a breath. "I swear I've gotten my days all mixed up before. My head is usually all over the place, so maybe I have this wrong, but it says here…yeah, it says Tate's out on vacation this week. Does that sound right?"

The officers meet my eyes across the table as I swallow, my throat dry. Nothing about this sounds right at all.

CHAPTER THREE

CELINE

When I finally leave the police station, the world is dark around me. I've spoken to every contact in my phone who would possibly know where Tate is, but no one gave us anything to go on.

To my surprise, his boss confirmed he took the week off for a last-minute vacation I had no knowledge of.

Which means every day this week he's left to go to work, and I have no idea where he ended up.

The police are holding on to his phone for now, searching it for anything that might help us, but I think we're all just sort of at a loss.

I vacillate between anger that he was lying to me this week, fear that something might be really wrong, and a state of overwhelm because I now have to deal with the police investigation, our car insurance, and telling the family and our boys something I don't understand myself, all while worrying about where he might be.

The tracking app on my phone shows that he went into work this morning and left around noon, but his coworkers have said he wasn't there. So where is he? Why did he take the week off? Who was the man driving his car? Why did he have his wallet and phone? And, maybe most peculiar, why do they share the same tattoo design, both on their right shoulders?

I'm no closer to having any answers when I arrive at my parents' house. The front door swings open at once, and both sets of parents flood out. My father is solemn, but everyone else has tears in their swollen, red eyes.

I step out of the car, trying desperately to hold it together, though I know it's no use.

"Where is he?" his mom demands, pulling me into a tight hug. "What did you find out? We went to the police station, but they wouldn't tell us anything."

When she leans back to look at me, I shake my head. "I…I don't know if there's anything to tell. No one knows where he is. I've called everyone I can think of to call. We can't find him." I glance toward the house. "Where are the boys?"

"Watching television," my mom says. "Your dad gave them some ice cream. They don't know what's going on. We haven't told them. Well, we didn't know *what* to tell them anyway. Lane and Daphne filled us in some, but…" She pauses, the skin around her eyes wrinkling with worry. "What's happening? What do you mean you can't find him?"

"The police called me today at work because they said Tate was involved in a car crash. They said...they told me he'd died in a crash...but when I got there, the photos they showed me weren't him."

"Photos?" Daphne asks, drying her eyes as more continue to fall. "What do you mean? They didn't let you see him?"

"Apparently that's how it works. It's supposed to...I don't know, make it easier on the family or something. Not having to..." I pause, collecting myself before I fall apart. "They just had photos," I say finally. "But...it was someone else. Someone else had been driving his car. Whoever it was, he had his cell phone and wallet, too."

"He was robbed," Lane says, his voice a low whisper. "Is that what they're thinking? They wouldn't tell us a thing. Took our numbers and said they'd be in touch." He scoffs. "How can they do that?"

I sigh, feeling the agony of the lack of answers in my bones. "I don't know. I brought that up too, suggested that maybe he'd been robbed, but there are... other things that make that less likely."

Every set of worried eyes lands on me.

"Other things?" Dad asks. "Like what?"

"Tate took the week off of work." I pick at the skin around my thumbnail. "He's been telling me he's going into the office all week, but he told his boss he was on vacation."

"Why would he do that?" Daphne asks, shaking her head with concern. "That doesn't sound like him."

"I don't know," I admit. "I checked his phone and went back as far as it would let me on the location app, and it looks like he was there every day."

"Sounds like a coverup," Lane says, staring into space. "The police need to speak to his boss. He has to be lying."

"They did speak to him. The company has given them security footage to comb through, but his coworkers are good people. I don't believe any of them would lie about this. I don't see any reason they'd have to do this."

"What about the man who was driving Tate's car? Was he a coworker?"

I press my lips together. "I don't think so. I knew all of the other agents at the firm. It could've been an assistant, but...the other weird thing is that they had matching tattoos."

Daphne's head tilts to the side. "What do you mean?"

I tap my shoulder, running a finger across the skin. "The lion on his shoulder. He...the man who died, he had a similar one."

"Well, that can't be a coincidence, can it? They must've known each other. What else could that mean?" Dad asks.

"I don't know," I say. "The police are supposed to

look into his clients and search his phone for any leads, but—"

"Mom!" Ryker rushes toward me, leaping off the porch. "Did you bring us anything?"

"What?" I gather him in my arms, hugging him against my chest. It always takes me by surprise that he's nearly as tall as I am at just ten years old.

"Grandma said you were shopping," he says, pulling back just in time for Finley to launch himself against me next. At seven, he's just a few inches shorter than his brother.

"Why don't we go inside, kids?" Mom says, holding out her arms. "All of us. I think we should give your mom a chance to get off her feet."

Really, she's giving me time to prepare what I'll say to them next, but no amount of time could ever be enough. Daphne takes my hand, and Lane takes hers, and we follow my parents and the boys up the walk and back into the house.

No one prepares you for this. There is no 'How to Tell Your Young Sons Their Father is Missing and Possibly Dead' manual out there on shelves, ready to walk you through the moment, step by step. Bit of a niche market, I suppose, but I'd buy up every copy in existence if it meant I had help doing this.

They know something is wrong. Everyone is crying

and holding hands as we stare down at them, trying to work out our next steps. I have to tell them something, even if it's not the entire truth just yet.

Especially when I don't know what that truth might be.

Finley sits on my lap while Ryker is next to me, tucked up under my arm. It's been a long time since he let me hold him like this—at ten, he's getting too old for snuggles with Mommy, though it breaks my heart. Still, something in this moment seems to tell him it's needed.

I kiss both of their heads, offering the most reassuring smile I can muster. They know nothing of death yet—all of their grandparents are alive and sitting here. The family dog, a brown-and-black cocker spaniel, is beginning to gray, but with any luck, he's still years away from the end of his life. I need Tate to be okay. They can't lose their dad first. I have to believe that he's alive out there somewhere, that he's okay, and that he's coming back to us. I have to believe we're going to find him because I'm not sure I could ever stop looking.

"So…" I puff out a breath of air. "I have some kind of confusing news, babies, but what I want to make sure you know first is that, no matter what, we're going to make it through this. We're going to be together, and we're going to be alright. And"—I look up, blinking away fresh tears to keep them from falling—"and you are so, so loved, okay? We all love you boys so very much."

They're just staring at me. Not saying or doing anything other than blinking and growing more confused by the moment. My mom's hand finds my back, and she rubs it just as she did when I was a child —an act that gives me more comfort than I've felt all day.

"So...there's a chance Daddy isn't, um, Daddy might not be coming home tonight, okay?" I pinch my lips together, my eyes stinging as I fight against the tears.

"What do you mean?" Ryker asks.

"Well, he's...he might be going away for a few days, or maybe longer." I sigh, scratching my forehead. "The truth is we don't know when he's coming back."

"Well, where is he?" Ryker is insistent, clearly annoyed at the lack of answers. I just don't want to break it to them yet. I have to hold on to hope, and if there's even a sliver of a chance that Tate will come home, I don't see a point in scaring them.

"We don't know. We don't think that anything bad happened, but he's just...away for a while." Tate's mom begins to cry silently, leaning against Lane's chest. "I'm sure that he's fine, sweetheart, but right now we all have to be very brave while we try to figure out where he might've gone and wait for him to come home, okay?" I take another breath as the words choke me, blowing it out slowly. In front of me, Finley's little chin has begun to quiver. "Can you do that for Mommy? Can you be brave?"

"Can't you just call him?" Ryker asks, his little

brows drawn down, searching for a solution that doesn't exist.

"Well, no." I run a hand over his cheek, wishing more than anything it was that simple. "I've—"

"Why not?" he demands.

"We've tried that, sweetheart. I've tried. He's not answering his phone."

"What does that mean?" Finley asks. "He always has his phone. He takes it to the bathroom with him." His lips upturn with a hopeful smile that shatters me.

"I don't really know." I snuggle him closer to me. "I wish that I did, but I don't. All I can tell you is that we're going to do everything we can to find him, okay? Mommy is going to do everything she can. And I'll tell you everything I can, but right now, we really don't know what any of it means. We don't know why he isn't here, but I know he wants to be. I know he'd never leave you, and I know he'll be home soon." Wishful thinking, perhaps, but I need to believe it as much as I need them to.

"Did Dad run away?" Ryker asks.

"Is he playing a game?" Finley adds, a hint of hope in his voice.

"I wish I knew, boys. We all do," I say, my voice sounding so small and frail it's practically a whisper. "But we aren't giving up on him, okay? We're all going to work so hard to find him, starting tonight. I'm going to take you home, and Grandma and Grandpa are going to stay with you while Mommy goes to look for him, okay?"

"What if he doesn't want to come home?" Ryker asks.

I open my mouth to answer, but think twice, changing direction. "Why would you ask that?"

He fiddles with a piece of loose string on his shirt.

"Did Daddy say something to you that made you think he might leave?" I run a hand over his back cautiously.

He shakes his head. "What if he's mad at us?"

The question shatters me, and I can't answer. I can't say anything.

My mom takes over, pulling Ryker against her. "Honey, your daddy loves you more than anything. I'll bet you, wherever he is, he's trying his hardest to get back to you."

She looks at me over his head, our eyes locked, and promises me the same silently, though we both know it might be a lie.

CHAPTER FOUR

CELINE

Back at my house, I've finally gotten the boys down in bed. In the kitchen, the grandparents wait at the table, talking through an endless loop of ideas. Daphne is on the phone with someone. I don't have the time to fall apart, so instead I formulate a plan.

As I reach the table, Daphne ends her call with a sigh. "That was Mary Ellen."

I don't recognize the name, but I don't say as much. I can hardly muster the awareness to think, let alone speak. I sit down at the head of the table, sinking my head into my hands. I feel completely empty. Numb. More and more, I find myself bargaining with the universe to just wake me up. That I'll do anything if I could just wake up from this nightmare.

"From my Bunco group," she reminds Lane. "She hasn't heard anything, but she's the first to know anything that happens in this town, so she's promised to ask around and keep an eye out."

"Okay, we need to do something," I say from behind my hands. "I'm going to call the detective on Tate's case again. He gave me his phone number at the station and said I could call for updates." I cross back into the living room and grab my purse from the couch, digging through it. I sort through snacks for the boys, a bottle of hand sanitizer, several pens, and my worn-out wallet before I find the card Detective Monroe gave me.

Holding the card, I type in his number and put the phone on speaker so everyone can hear the conversation.

"Monroe." He answers with a single word.

"Um, hi." My voice is shaking, and I hate it. "This... this is Celine Thompson." Suddenly standing by my side, Daphne puts a hand on my shoulder, giving me a reassuring smile. "I'm calling to ask for an update about my husband's case. Tate, um, Tatum Thompson."

There's a beat of silence before we get an answer. "Mrs. Thompson, thanks for checking in. As of right now, we're still sorting through the evidence from your husband's phone and work computer. I went down to his office right after we met to speak with his coworkers and get a clearer picture of his movements. I apologize for not getting a chance to call you sooner."

"What did they say?" I ask.

"More of what we already knew. Tate put in for this vacation just last week, which leads me to believe whatever is going on, something caused this to happen quickly. Was there anything abnormal about his behavior last week?"

I pinch my bottom lip between my fingers, thinking. *The text.* If I tell them about the text, will it make me look suspicious? I swallow. "No. Not that I can think of."

The detective hums. "Well, we're still working through some theories and trying to get a timeline together of the past few days for him. I'll be in touch as soon as we have any updates."

Yeah, just like you were this time.

"Should we be doing anything?" Daphne asks. "Is there anything we can do to help?"

"Who is that?" the detective asks.

"Tate's mom," I say. "Daphne Thompson."

"Good evening, Mrs. Thompson," he says. "As of right now, as hard as it is, my best advice is the same I've already given Celine. Stay put, keep your focus on anything you might have overlooked the past week or so, and let us know if you hear from Tate. I know you want to do more, but the best we can do for Tate right now is putting our heads together and looking for a break in his usual pattern or behavior. Something caused him to take that vacation and something has caused him to go missing. Soon, we'll break the story to the media, but we don't want to risk the progress we've made by spooking anyone just yet."

"Spooking anyone?" Daphne asks, her voice quivering. "You mean if someone has him held captive?"

"We don't have any reason to believe your son is in danger, ma'am. We're hoping to know more soon, and we'll be in touch as soon as we do."

Daphne doesn't look pleased, but she says nothing else as I thank the detective and end the call. With a sigh, I join them at the table again.

When I do, Lane huffs. "They're treating him as if he's the one in the wrong here, not this criminal who stole his car."

Mom reaches out, taking my hand and rubbing it with hers. "What can we do?"

Without looking up, I shake my head. "I don't know. You heard the police. They don't want us to do anything apparently. They told me earlier they're going to use his phone to get data about his recent activities and they're supposed to be looking up surveillance footage, but…" A puff of air escapes my chest. "That doesn't feel like enough. We need to contact people. We need to search—"

"We've been calling everyone who might know anything," Daphne says, her eyes filled with worry. "I just don't have his coworkers' numbers, but you spoke with his boss, didn't you?"

I nod. "Well, I talked to Dustin, the receptionist, not his boss, but why would he have taken the week off without telling me? That's the thing I can't make sense of. Why would he lie?" I look at both of his parents then, feeling guilty for asking but hoping they'll have an answer.

They exchange a glance, though neither seems able to come up with a response that would make sense without making their son look like a liar.

I'm so angry with him, but I have no idea what I'm angry about. I'm worried and upset and furious that I'm in this situation—that I don't even fully understand what this situation is. Where is Tate? Who was the man in the car? What in the world is going on?

Surely the police will figure it out soon. I want to believe it, but it would be a lie to say I don't have doubts. Surely they'll get answers, but...what if they don't? What if I just never learn anything? What if Tate has just...vanished? What if I never see him again?

I need to do something. Anything.

A pang of sadness rebounds in my heart, and even surrounded by the people I love, I feel wholly alone.

"There will be some sort of explanation," Daphne says, reaching across the table to stroke my arm.

"Of course there will," Lane agrees. "He's alright. He's fine." His words sound more like he's trying to reassure himself than me. "He's going to be back home in no time at all, you'll see."

"We need to search. Go to restaurants he likes or... places he goes. Something." Even as I say it, I know it's useless. My husband is a homebody. He spends his time with us. Aside from work, he goes almost nowhere else. "I can't just sit here and do nothing. I don't care what the police say."

Mom scrapes her hand across her forehead like she always does when she's thinking hard. "I agree. Daphne and I were just saying we should organize some sort of search party. We could canvas the neighborhood or... what are you thinking? "

The truth is, I don't know. The police haven't given me any sort of instructions or guidance on how to handle this situation other than to sit here twiddling my thumbs as if I'm helpless. I'm alone and in uncharted waters, and I have no idea what any of this means or what I should be doing.

"I don't know," I say softly, dusting a tear from my cheek. I sniffle, brushing away another one as it falls. "They didn't tell me anything except to wait to hear more from them once they go through his phone, just like you heard. They said to contact anyone who might know where he is, but we've done that. Tate didn't have a huge circle. It's just us." I look around the room, knowing this is our whole circle. If I were to go missing, these are the people who would look for me too. "I just need to get out and drive. Look for him. I need to go."

"Go where?" Mom asks.

"You shouldn't be out on your own." Dad's voice leaves no room for negotiation. "I know you want to do something, but we need a plan. You can't just go driving around without any idea where you're going or

32

why. It's the middle of the night at this point. We'll stay. To help with the boys or be here if you need to leave, but let's be smart about this. You're upset, and I know you have every right to be, but you're not in a state to drive. You look ready to pass out."

"Can you blame her?" Daphne balks. "What are we supposed to do? The police aren't telling us anything! You heard that detective. They all but blamed Tate for disappearing, as if he kidnapped himself."

Dad flattens his hands on the table, his voice level. "We need to stay calm. We'll make a list of everyone you haven't talked to already who might have heard from Tate. There has to be someone else. His clients, maybe? Tonight, we can start calling them, and in the morning, we'll visit his office and—"

"No. We can't call his clients." My tone is harsher than I mean for it to be.

"Why not?" Mom asks.

"First of all, because all of their information is in his phone, which I don't have. There might be some at the office, but I couldn't legally access it. And, second of all, because it would look wholly unprofessional—"

"Who cares?" Mom's eyes wrinkle in the corners as she studies me, and finally, her chest puffs with a deep breath.

"Tate would care," I say firmly. "He *does* care. He's worked so hard for his career. We can't embarrass him." I know there's so much unspoken in the room right now. None of us know if Tate will come back for the career he's worked so hard for, but I have to believe I'm right about this. If I embarrass him in front of his clients or bring them into our family drama, he might never forgive me. "The police will contact them if they think it's necessary, but for now, we have to come up with something else."

"There's no one else to contact," Lane says with a broken, exhausted tone. "Nowhere else to go. We have to talk to his boss. Find out more about this vacation he took. When did he ask for it off? What did he tell him?"

I lick my lips and pull out my phone, grateful for any sort of plan. I don't have Tate's boss's phone number saved in my contacts, but a quick internet search gives it to me, and I click on it, placing the call. It rings once and goes to voicemail.

I sigh. It's late. I hadn't expected any different, but still. I leave a quick message and ask him to call me back. I have no idea if any of this is allowed. Am I interfering with a police investigation somehow? Will I get into trouble?

Interrupting my racing thoughts, Mom speaks up. "Why don't you go to bed? You're exhausted. There's nothing else that can be done tonight, and you'll feel better in the morning."

"I can't go to bed," I tell her, shaking my head. "My husband is missing. *Tate* is…he's missing." My voice cracks, and I feel the last bit of my resolve crumbling. Tate isn't coming home tonight. He may not be coming home ever. He's just gone. He's really, truly gone.

Mom stands up from the table, gathering me in her arms without a word, and I rest my head against her, silent tears streaming down my cheeks. I don't know how I'm supposed to feel or what I'm supposed to say. I just want answers. I just want to understand.

"Lane and I will start calling around to hospitals," Daphne says, her voice soft and mousy through tears of her own. "Just in case, you know? Someone has to know something." With that, they stand and back out of the room, leaving me alone with my parents.

When they've left, Mom pulls away from me slightly, clasping my cheeks between her hands. She just stares at me for a long while, her eyes glassy and unreadable, and I know she's trying desperately to be strong for me like she always has. "There's nothing you can do tonight, Celine," she says finally. "The police are doing all they can, and if you want, we can get up at dawn and start searching, make more phone calls, but for now...for now you have to sleep." When I start to argue, she holds up a hand, cutting me off. "You have to *rest*, even if you can't sleep."

"Is that what you'd do if it were me? If I were missing, would you guys just go to bed?" There is nothing hateful in my tone. Even if I felt angry with my parents —which I don't—I don't have the strength to summon anything but emptiness.

She doesn't seem to have an answer to that, so she

releases my cheeks and exchanges a worried glance with my father. "Sweetheart, there's nothing else you can do. It's late. People aren't answering their phones. It's too dark to see to search, too late to bother neighbors. I know you're worried, and we are too, but you've done absolutely everything you can do tonight. I have to believe Tate would want you to take care of yourself and the boys. You can't run yourself ragged when nothing else can be done tonight. The police are working. You need to rest."

"Fine," I say softly, rubbing my eyes. "I'll go to bed."

Their eyes dart back toward me.

"I'll go to bed and try to come up with a plan for tomorrow. I'm not saying I'll sleep because we all know I won't, but I need to think and run through everything in my head. Process. I know him. If I think about it hard enough, surely I can come up with a few places we haven't already thought to look for him, people we haven't called."

Dad nods, moving toward us and putting a hand on Mom's shoulder. "I think that's a smart plan. Do you want us to stay?"

"No," I tell him as gently as I can. "Thank you for offering. I love you, and I appreciate it, but I just...I need to be alone right now."

Dad starts to say something, probably to argue, but Mom cuts him off. "We'll let Lane and Daphne know. And we'll be back in the morning. You call us if you need anything, okay? We can be back over here in twenty minutes. I'll keep my phone on." Mom always sleeps with her phone on Do Not Disturb because the slightest sound or light wakes her, so I know she's saying she won't be sleeping much either. Somehow, that makes me feel a little better. I hug them both. Then, completely wiped out by exhaustion, I disappear down the hall and into our bedroom without a word to my in-laws. I don't want to have to explain to them why I'm going to bed. I don't have the strength to hold the weight of their judgment right now, but I also won't blame them if they do judge me. They should. Going to bed is the last thing I should be doing, yet my body refuses to do anything else.

When I hear their car doors shut moments later and then spot their headlights shining through the curtains, I breathe a sigh of relief. Then, just as quickly, the tears begin to fall.

I curl up in my bed, trying my hardest to stifle the sounds of my sobs so I don't wake the boys, covering my mouth so hard I feel as if I'm suffocating myself. My body hurts from holding in the pain, but I have to be strong for them, even if I'm faking every second of the display.

After an hour has passed, and I'm no longer crying, just lying on my side across the bed with cool tears cascading across my nose and onto my temple, I hear a noise. A sound draws me from the trance I'm in, though it takes several seconds for me to recognize what it is.

In my purse on the floor, my phone is vibrating.

I assume it's my mother, calling to say good night or check in, but when I see the words on the screen, my heart stalls.

Unknown Caller

I consider not answering it for a split second, toying with the idea of letting it go to voicemail, but even if the situation with Tate didn't have my interest, the late hour would. As many spam calls as I get, none of them come in the middle of the night.

Without another thought, I swipe my finger across the screen to answer it. Could this be *the* call? The ransom demand? The explanation? The apology?

What am I supposed to say? Police always prepare you for these in the movies, but no one has prepared me at all. I'm going to mess this up somehow.

"Hello?" My voice shakes as I answer, and if the person doesn't know what's going on, if they aren't calling about Tate, they might assume I've been sleeping.

I listen as the other end of the line lingers in silence. Ordinarily, I'd have hung up already, but now I can't afford to. I have no way to know if this is related to Tate, but if it is, I need to keep the line open. I need the person to know I'm listening.

"Hello? Is anyone there?"

Still, nothing. Radio silence.

"Tate?" I whisper, my voice cracking under the weight of that syllable. A sound, an utterance, that feels as old hat to me as brushing my teeth or blinking. "Are you there?"

Then I hear it. A single exhalation. A breath caught in the air. Someone has released a breath. There is an actual living, breathing person on the line, but they don't want me to know it.

Or maybe they can't make a sound.

"Tate, honey? Is that you? If...if it is...breathe out again." Maybe his captor is close by. Maybe I'm putting him at risk to ask him to make a single noise.

If so, he's safe. Because there are no other noises, and soon enough, the line goes dead.

CHAPTER FIVE

TATE

Eight Days Before Disappearance

Celine is already home by the time I get there. Inside, the house is quiet and smells of dinner. I make my way through the house, half expecting them to be hiding or pretending to be asleep so they can jump up and scare me as they so often do whenever I enter the house at the end of the day.

Instead, I find my plate of chicken and rice casserole waiting on the counter and no sign of my family. The food smells delicious, and my stomach growls on sight. I skipped lunch today, and I'm feeling the results of that. Celine likes to sneak broccoli into this particular casserole and coat it with enough cheese the kids don't notice. Leaning down over the plate, I take a small bite and notice it's cool, but not yet cold. She recently set it out.

The casserole dish is still waiting on the stovetop, and I can feel the heat from it before my hand touches the surface. The time on the stove tells me it's just after seven, so not quite bedtime.

"Guys?" I call, spinning around. *Are they planning to try and scare me?*

I make my way down the hallway toward the bedrooms when I spot the light on in the bathroom. As I get closer, I can hear the water running, and my chest floods with a warm relief.

I push the door open cautiously. "Anyone home?"

"Dad!" Finley calls, leaning his little blond head out of the bathtub and waving at me, his arm coated and dripping with bubbles. Ryker is in front of the bathtub with a towel wrapped around his waist the way I showed him, running a comb methodically through his hair. There's a new girl at school he's been talking about a lot lately—Asha. Since he started talking about her, I've noticed he's been spending a lot more time getting ready.

My chest goes warm at the thought. I can't believe we're already here. I know everyone says it goes by fast, but until you live it, those words don't do the experience justice.

Celine is sitting on the toilet lid across from the bathtub, grinning broadly at me. Her long, dark curls are everywhere, sticking to her neck from the humidity of the room, the front pieces brushed back out of her face without care. She's as beautiful and unconcerned with that beauty as ever.

"Hey, baby," she says, grinning as she tilts her mouth up for me to press a kiss to her lips when I approach her.

"Hey there."

"Finley has something to tell you." She nods her head toward our son, who is waiting anxiously for me to make my way across the bathroom toward him. He grins up as I approach, and I see the news he has before he says the words.

"I lost another tooth!" Proudly, he pushes his tongue through the hole next to his newly grown-in front teeth.

"I see that." With a chuckle, I pat his head and squat down next to the bathtub for a better look. I squint, leaning in, then pull back and pin him with a look of concern. "Who said you were allowed to do that?"

"No one," he says, clearly confused. "It just happened."

"You're supposed to stop growing so fast, remember?"

Catching onto my joke, his head cocks to the side, and he gives me a patronizing look. "*Daaad.*"

I laugh, rubbing my hand over his hair again. "Just kidding, bud. Guess that means the tooth fairy is finally going to bring you the money you owe me for that candy at the store the other day, right?"

He hesitates. "Well…"

"He's kidding, Fin," Celine tells him with a playful eye roll.

I approach Ryker from behind, staring at him in the mirror. "How was your day, kiddo?"

"Fine," he grumbles, mouth full of toothpaste. After spitting it out, he turns to face me. "I need your help with my math homework."

"You've got it. Let me take a quick shower, and I'll meet you in your room after, okay?"

"Yep." He turns back toward the mirror while I face Celine.

"I'll be right back."

She grins. "No problem. I left your dinner out, too."

"I saw it, thanks. I'll heat it back up after I help him with homework." I squeeze her shoulder gently as I pass her and head for our bedroom. In our bathroom, I strip out of my clothes and turn the shower on, peeing while I wait for the shower to heat up.

I'm exhausted, my body sore and my mind over-worked. Work has been brutal lately, and then I've had all the recent extra stress on top of it. I just can't seem to catch a break.

Once my shower is done, I step out, wrapping the towel around my waist before combing my hair. In the bedroom, I'm dressing when the door opens and Celine walks in.

She lies down on the bed with a sigh, running her hands over her eyes. I pull my shirt over my head and lie down next to her, massaging her thigh gently.

"Rough day?"

She turns her head to look at me with that same deliriously happy look that's almost always on her face. It never gets old when she looks at me that way, when I know I've caused it. "No, I'm just exhausted. How was your day?"

"Fine." I run my hand up her leg, over her hip, and up her side, stopping at her shoulder to twist one of her dark curls around my finger. "Sorry I was late."

"It's fine. Gave me just enough time to send my boyfriend home." She winks, and I drop my jaw in feigned shock, digging my fingers into her waist to tickle her.

"What did I tell you would happen if I saw him around here again?" I tease as she squeals.

Fighting for breath, she wrenches my hand away. "Okay, okay. I'll tell him to stay away for good this time."

"You'd better." I run my nose over hers, brushing her mouth with my lips.

"Anyway, better late than never." She leans into my lips, letting her mouth linger on mine for a moment longer than necessary. I put a hand on the back of her head and tug her flush against me in a single move. Pressing a hand against my chest, she pulls back. "Easy there, tiger. Ryker still needs your help with his home-work, and I need to do the dishes and read a few more chapters of *The Wild Robot* with Finley."

"Ah, right. Life still exists out there. How could I

forget?" I chuckle, running a hand over my face before adjusting my pants. I prop up on one elbow. "I can do the dishes," I tell her.

She stifles a yawn and rolls onto her back, looking over at me. "Are you sure?"

"You look exhausted."

A snort escapes her. "Gee, thanks."

"Beautiful." I lean over and kiss her forehead before standing up from the bed. "But exhausted. Go read to Finley while I help Ryker, then I'll eat and finish the dishes. You should get some rest."

She looks like she might argue but decides against it. "Okay. Thanks."

With that, I squeeze her knee gently and leave the room.

Ryker and I are nearly done with his math home-work when the door opens and Celine peeks inside. She crosses her arms with a grin, but it's different. Distant. Tired, maybe, but still unsettling. "How's it going in here?"

"Almost done," Ryker says.

"Multiplying and dividing fractions," I explain. "If I never have to look at another fraction, I'll be okay with that."

"Me too," Ryker agrees.

"Well, I'm afraid you have a few more years of 'em, bud," I say, pointing at the page to tell him to continue.

Celine's smile is stiff, her eyes staring off into the room at nothing at all.

"Everything okay?" I ask gently.

She senses the change in my tone and looks up, her bright, brown eyes searching mine. "Of course. Can I talk to you for a minute?"

"Yeah." I hop up, a stone sinking in my stomach. Has something happened to Finley? Or the house? The car? "I'll be right back, Ryk. Keep working."

He nods without looking up from his paper, the eraser of his pencil stuck between his teeth as he chomps down on it in thought. Celine pushes the bedroom door open, disappearing out of it without needing to instruct me to follow her. She leads the way toward our bedroom, and when I step inside, she spins around, arms folded across her chest.

"Is something wrong?" I venture a guess.

"I don't know," she says, her harsh tone foreign. "Is there something you need to tell me?"

"Um…" I search my brain. There's no way she knows about anything, so I have no idea what she's talking about or why I seem to be in trouble. "I don't think so." I force a soft, breathy laugh.

She reaches behind her, and I spot my phone lying on the edge of the bed moments before she picks it up. My chest goes icy as I try to remember if I might've left anything on it that would make her mad at me. It's not like Celine to go through my phone. I can't remember the last time I touched hers.

"I was trying to go to bed, and your phone lit up. I thought it might be a client or something important, so

46

I checked it." She nudges the phone toward me, a text message lighting up the screen.

The message is from a number I don't recognize, but the message tells me who it is without needing to think about it.

You need to tell her.

CHAPTER SIX

CELINE

When I wake up the next morning, my head is pounding with an ache that tells me I've both slept too hard and simultaneously not gotten enough sleep.

I called the detective right after receiving that strange phone call, but there wasn't much to be done about it. He said they'd see about getting the phone company to track it, but without any sort of threat or known crime, it's likely he won't get the request approved. He told me to contact him if there is another call and to try to keep them on the line as long as possible, to listen for any defining sounds that might give us a hint as to their location if it does have something to do with Tate. Then, with a metaphorical pat on the head, he sent me on my way to deal with another element of confusion in my already confusing situation.

I can hear the sounds of people talking down the

hall and quickly realize it's my parents speaking to the boys. I roll over and glance at the time. It's just after six. I wasn't expecting them here so early.

I pick up my phone, checking to see if the mysterious number called back, but there isn't anything important on the screen. Just a few social media notifications that amount to nothing. I don't have the energy to even open them.

Rubbing my eyes, I slip out of bed. The day already feels heavy. So heavy I'm half tempted to jump back into bed, wrap up in the covers, and dissolve.

But I can't. Not only because I still have to pretend I have a shred of my life together for the boys' sake but also because I haven't yet let Margie know what is happening, and I'm scheduled for a shift at eight.

In the bathroom, I brush my teeth and study my face in the mirror. My eyes are red and puffy, both from crying and from lack of sleep, and my skin is practically gray. I look like someone who is rotting from the inside out, and I don't feel far from it.

I can't help thinking, somewhat bitterly, about how different this might be if the situation were reversed. Tate would be allowed to stay in bed all day and not a soul would judge him for it. But moms are not afforded the luxury of falling apart, even during the worst of times.

With a fresh set of clothes on and my hair pulled back in a loose ponytail at the nape of my neck, I only feel ninety-eight percent like garbage, which is an improvement, as I step out into the hallway.

Dad's there, searching under the bench for a pair of shoes. He looks up as if he's surprised to see me. "Morning, honey. I hope we didn't wake you." He stands up and slips a hand around my shoulders when I approach him. Leaning over, he kisses the side of my head.

"I didn't sleep much," I say, resting my head on his shoulder. "What are you guys doing here so early?"

He drops his hand from my shoulder, and we step apart. "We came to get the boys ready for school. Your mom thought we should take them and let you get some sleep if you could." Bending back down as he apparently spots the match to the shoe he'd been looking for, he snags it, then heads into the living room.

"I wasn't planning on sending them."

Before he can respond, Mom sees us and darts out of the kitchen and into the living room to meet us. The boys are at the kitchen table, eating bowls of what I assume is oatmeal from the smell that has permeated the entire house.

"You didn't wake her up. I told you not to wake her up," Mom says, then looks at me before she gets an answer. "He didn't wake you up, did he?"

"No," we answer at the same time.

Mom huffs a breath and studies me. "We were trying to be quiet."

"I know. I barely slept. I didn't think you guys would be here so early." My eyes flick toward the boys in the living room. "I wasn't planning on sending them to school today."

"I didn't figure you were, but I think they should go." She crosses her arms, lowering her voice even more. "Right now, all there is for them to do is worry. Going to school will distract them. Let them go until we know more."

I swallow. She's right. I know she's right, but I also know if I let them out of my sight, there's a chance I might not see them again. I let Tate walk away from me to go to work one time, and now, that may have been the last time I'll ever see him.

How can I ever let the boys leave my sight again?

"It's going to be okay," Mom says softly. "Just...let's let them be kids a bit longer." Her voice is suddenly thick and strained, her eyes gleaming with tears. She thinks he's gone. She thinks we're just waiting for the news to arrive. *Am I foolish for thinking he's still alive? That he might still come home?*

With a single glance at my boys at the kitchen table, I know she's right. Last night I told them it was going to be okay. I told them their father was going to come home eventually. For now, they still believe me. They trust me.

If I'm wrong, I'll never get that trust back. Never again will they so blindly take my word for anything. Until we know something for certain, I need to let their lives remain unchanged. Routine and consistency are the only things we have going for us right now.

"Yeah. Okay. You're right."

She huffs a breath of relief. "What can we do to help after we've dropped them off?"

"I'm going to his office," I say. "Could you guys stay at the house in case he shows up? And get the boys from school for me?"

"Of course," Mom says. "Is that really all you need?"

"Yeah, for now. It's as far as I've gotten with my plan. I'm hoping I'll know more once I talk to his boss."

"Let me come with you," Dad says. "You still don't look like you need to be driving."

"I'll be fine," I promise him. "Honestly. I just want to handle this alone. It's a huge help to know you've got the boys."

He looks hesitant but eventually agrees. "Whatever you need."

I nod, making my way into the kitchen to tell the boys good morning.

"Morning, Mom," Finley says. "I had the dream about the mice again." Lately, Finley has been dreaming about mice coming into his bedroom in the night and climbing under the covers with him.

I pat his head, slipping into the chair next to him. "Morning, bud. Did you scare them away?"

"No, not this time. They were nice mice." He shovels a spoonful of oatmeal into his mouth.

"There's no such thing as nice mice, is there, Mom?" Ryker asks skeptically.

I shrug, too tired for conversations about mice personalities, but I push ahead anyway. "I don't think mice are inherently bad. They're just trying to survive, like the rest of us. We just don't want them in our house."

"Some people have pet mice," Finley says.

"That's true." I pat the table and do my best to form a convincing smile. "Are you both ready for school?"

"What about Dad?" Ryker asks. "Will he be here when we get home?"

It takes me a second to form an answer that isn't a lie, but also won't destroy them. "I hope so," I say finally. "But I don't want you guys to worry about that, okay? I just want you to focus on having a good day and let Mommy deal with the rest of it."

"I hope Dad gets home soon," Finley says. "I want to tell him about my dream."

"I hope so too, pumpkin." I stand and pick up his empty bowl, kissing his cheek and then Ryker's, and take their dishes to the sink. "You boys should get your shoes on, okay? Grandma and Grandpa will get you to school, and then I'll see you this afternoon."

Moments later, on their way out the door, Finley turns back to me, studying me with an incredulous expression.

"What is it, bud?"

He hesitates again. "When…um, when we get home today, you'll be here, right?"

A ball of dough lodges in my throat as I drop to my knees in front of him. "Yes. Yes, Mommy will be here. I promise." I squeeze him tight, blinking back tears. "I love you so much."

"I love you, too." He hugs my neck, then slips away, taking my mom's hand on the way to the car. I watch as they buckle the boys in and then disappear down the driveway with tears pouring down my cheeks. With Tate gone, everything feels more consequential. Dramatic. Real.

As if I'm saying goodbye to them forever just because they've left my sight.

I force the thought away—*I'm being ridiculous. I'm not saying goodbye.* They'll be back this afternoon. I'm simply sending them to school so they aren't subjected to the same turmoil and stress I will be dealing with today. And every day, for that matter, until we learn the truth about where Tate is and what is going on.

And that's what I'll be dedicating today to. But first I head back to our bedroom, where I find my phone and look up Margie's number in my contacts. When her cell phone goes to a voicemail box that's full, I assume she didn't answer because she's at the shop already and call that number instead.

"Thanks for calling The Bold Bean, this is Jerry. How can I help you?" comes the voice of one of the newest employees.

"Jerry, this is Celine Thompson. Is Margie there?"

"Well, howdy there, Celine." For no apparent reason, while at work, the kid talks like he's a sixty-year-old cowboy rather than a twenty-one-year-old skateboarder, but we've all learned to ignore it. "She sure is. Let me track 'er down for ya, okay? Just a second."

Within literal seconds, Margie is on the line. "Celine? What's going on? Are you coming in today?"

"No. I'm sorry, but I need to take the day off," I tell her. "All the stuff with my husband and the police is still going on, and…" I come up with a lie on the spot. "I need to go down to the police station later and talk to them some more."

"Do you need the whole day off?"

"Yes," I say firmly. I'm the best employee she has, present moment excluded. The only one who has been there more than a year. I know there's no chance she's going to fire me or make me upset. "I'm not sure how long it's going to take, and besides that, we have a lot going on. Actually, I think I'd better go ahead and take the week off. Tate's missing, and I'm not really in a state to work."

She doesn't bother to hide her sigh, but eventually she says, "Whatever you need, honey. Just keep me updated, okay? I'll cover what I can and have Sophie or Jerry pick up the rest. They need the hours anyway. But if you want to come back earlier, just let me know."

"Right. I will. Okay, well, thanks."

"Yep." We haven't even ended the call when I hear her saying, "What can I get for ya, honey?"

With that taken care of, I hurry to our closet and change into my clothes for the day. I'm going to get answers today, one way or another.

Less than an hour later, I pull up in front of Tate's office. Morris Realty is a real estate firm that sits in the heart of downtown, in a building eight stories high and full of different businesses, all employing mostly men with perfectly coiffed hair and freshly whitened teeth.

Tate's office is on the third floor, but when I enter, I'm stopped at the door by a guard who asks where I'm going and searches my bag. When he's done and I'm cleared, I make my way up to the office and spot Dustin behind the large, circular desk in the center of the room.

His uneasy grin tells me he hasn't forgotten our phone call from yesterday.

"Hi, Celine." He stands, moving the headset mic away from in front of his mouth. "We weren't expecting you. How are you?" He walks around the desk and stops in front of me with an empathetic stare. I like Dustin, really I do. He and his husband are the two people I always spend the most time talking to at the office parties. But at this exact moment? I want to claw his eyeballs out with my bare hands.

"I need to be let inside Tate's office, please."

He clasps his hands together in front of him. "Right. Sure." Stepping back, he makes his way around the desk and grabs a set of keys from his top drawer, then leads the way down the hall. I'm surprised it's this easy, honestly. "The police were here yesterday evening," he tells me, almost conspiratorially.

"They were?" I try to sound shocked, hoping Dustin will tell me something Detective Monroe left out.

He nods, stopping at the door and sliding the key into the lock.

"Did they find anything?"

"I don't think so." He swings the door open. "They copied his hard drive or something techy like that and took a few pictures of his desk and some of the note-books he had lying around, I guess with notes and stuff in them." As I step into the office, he follows behind me, standing in the doorway. "Have they told you anything?"

I chew my bottom lip. "No, nothing at all. Which is why I'm here." I stop behind his desk. "He really wasn't here all week?"

He sticks his head out into the hallway at the sound of a voice, then turns back to meet my gaze. "Sorry, what?"

"Tate. You said he wasn't here all week, right?"

He nods slowly. "Well, yeah. He said he was on vacation, that you guys were going to work on some projects around the house or something like that. He came in a few different times, but always left right after. I guess he was just picking something up." His expression is full of guilt. "I hope it's okay that I'm telling you this. I don't want to get him into trouble. I'm sure there's some explanation."

"Right now, all I want to do is find my husband and make sure he's okay," I say simply. "I promise I'm not planning to rat you out. Whatever you tell me will stay between us." I sink into the office chair and tug open one of the drawers. The top one is full of only pens, pencils, sticky notes, and breath mints. The second one is locked. I look at Dustin, who is staring back out into the hallway.

"Do you happen to have a key for these drawers?"

"Um…" He hesitates. "I do, but it's locked in the key box, and I can't get to it without a number two."

I stare at him, not understanding.

He rushes to explain. "I'm a number one. The key box has two separate combos, and you need a one and a two to open it. Tim's the only other person here right now, and we're both ones. Everyone else is out. Kaira was here yesterday to open the drawers for the police, but she's out on showings right now and Matt's at a training." He winces. "I'm sorry."

"It's okay," I say with a huff. When he glances back out into the hallway for a third time, I add, "You can go if you need to. I'll let you know when I'm done in here."

He winces. "I…actually, I can't. Only employees are allowed in the offices, just because there's client information on the computers and stuff, and well, I mean obviously I trust you and know you aren't doing anything sketchy"—he gives a nervous laugh—"but I have to stay with you."

"I can't even get into anything." I gesture toward the computer, which is locked. "I'm just looking to see if he left anything that could help me find him." I tug at the next drawer, which is also locked.

Dustin gives a regretful, one-sided smile, but he doesn't respond. Realizing he's not going to leave, I pull at the next drawer, which is also locked, and then turn toward the other side of the L-shaped desk. Like its twin, this side's top drawer is unlocked, but its contents are wholly unhelpful. Two protein bars, a stack of business cards, a blank notepad, a basket of paper clips, a stapler, and a single roll of tape are all that await me. The next two drawers are locked.

Thinking quickly, I grab a sheet of paper from his printer and a pencil and place it over the blank notepad, shading lightly across the paper to see if there's an address or note that might point me in the right direction.

Dustin watches me intently, but to my disappointment, there are just a few notes jotted down that I'm able to make out.

> 4 beds
> Comps for Odessa??
> yard space + easy commute

210k
890k
Commission split?
Bathrooms
Two story—no go

None of it means anything suspicious to me.

With a sigh, I toss the paper into the trash can before reaching for the computer, cutting a glance at Dustin to see if he's going to stop me. When he says nothing, I move the mouse to wake the screen and begin to run through Tate's roster of passwords.

Our anniversary.

The boys' birthdays.

His birthday.

Nothing. Nothing. Nothing.

Each time, I'm met with the same error message.

Invalid credentials. Please try again.

"Did the police get into his computer?"

"I'm not really sure," he says. "I wasn't in here with them. Tim was. No one has his password, though, obviously, so if they did, they must've done some system override thing."

I sigh, gathering my face in my hands. The last thing I need to do is fall apart right now, but that's exactly what I feel is coming. "Is Tim with someone?" I ask.

"Uh…" Dustin's eyes shift toward the door again. "His next meeting isn't until ten."

"That's plenty of time." I stand up and cross the room, marching out of the office on the way to see Tate's boss. When I reach his door, he's on the phone, his loud voice booming across the office, as muffled as a pilot's voice before takeoff through the thick glass windows and closed door.

I knock softly, and when he eventually looks up, I wave.

His face visibly pales, and he says something into the phone before placing it down and standing up. Seconds later, he pulls the door open and stares at me. "Celine." The word is an apology, though I have no idea what he's apologizing for.

"I need you to tell me what you told the police about Tate."

He steps back, running a hand over his flat stomach. "Please. Come inside."

I do as he says, stepping into the office and taking a seat in front of his desk.

When he sits down in front of me, he smooths his hands out over the desk. "We're all just so sorry to hear about this mess with Tate."

"Dustin said he told you he was on vacation this week. And the detective on the case mentioned that you said he didn't tell you about needing time off until last week."

He nods, running a hand over his chin. "Yeah, yeah. That's right. He mentioned you guys had some home projects you were hoping to get done and they couldn't wait any longer."

I rub my lips together. "But his phone showed he came here all week. That he was here all day Monday and Tuesday and then left around noon yesterday, just before the crash."

Tim's face falls slightly. "Well, I'm not sure what to say about that. I only know what I told the police, which is that I haven't seen him since Friday."

"Did he take trips like this often?"

"Vacations?"

I nod.

"No, just once a year. Every summer, like clock-work. This was the first time he'd asked for time off when the kids were in school. I just thought...well, everybody needs extra time off now and again, and he's more than earned it. Plus, if you guys are fixing the place up to sell..." He gives a crooked grin that falls away quickly when I don't return it.

Every summer, we spend a week at his parents' beach house in Wilmington, NC. He hasn't lied a single time. This isn't common for him. *So what changed? Why did he lie now? What is going on?*

I keep going back to the text message, but his explanation made sense. I don't want to believe he lied about that too, but now? What am I supposed to think? I have to question everything, doubt everything, and I hate it more than I can say.

I hate the person this situation is turning me into.

"Was he acting strangely?" I ask. "Did anything seem

off about him?" These are the same questions I've been asking myself. The questions I desperately want answers to but can't seem to find. Because as far as I could tell, aside from the weird "Tell her" text message, nothing about my husband's behavior was off in the days or weeks leading up to his disappearance.

"No, nothing. He was his same old self, just like I told that detective. He'd been completely normal. No red flags."

I fold my hands together. "Last week he told me he'd had an appraisal come in low on a project one of your investment clients had sunk quite a bit of money into. He was really nervous to tell her because he said she was one of your biggest clients. The buyer's agent had texted him about telling the client their offer was going to change pretty drastically. I know it made him stressed out, and he was worried he'd lose their business. Do you know anything about that?"

His eyes drift around the room, clearly buying himself time to think, but eventually they find me again. "I can't say that it rings a bell off the top of my head, but none of the guys keep me up to date on every project, so—"

"It sounded like this would've been a major project."

"I can't say that I know about it, Celine. I'm sorry. I wish I did. That's par for the course in this business. Tate knew how to handle the bad with the good, and I'm sure he made it work. But we both know Tate shouldn't have been telling you clients' business, anyway. Maybe it's a little bit of a gray area we all tend to overlook when it's harmless, but with all of this going on, I can't tell you anything legally, even if I wanted to."

"So you do know something?"

"I didn't say that." He checks his Apple Watch, then stands. "I have a meeting coming up that I need to prepare for. Listen, if I hear from Tate, you'll be the first to know, okay? No one's praying for his safe return more than we are." He holds out his arm, gesturing toward the door. I'm half tempted to argue, but we both know I'm not going to get anywhere with his guard up.

Instead, I stand and meet his eyes. "Thanks for all your help, Tim. I really appreciate it."

"No problem," he tells me. "You guys are like family. You know that. Our thoughts and prayers are with you all, truly." With that, he gestures again that I should leave, and I step out of his office just before he shuts the door.

Back in the lobby, I tell Dustin goodbye and head for the elevator, feeling deflated. I thought for sure I'd find something here, but the only thing I've learned so far is that the police have already been here, and that from what I can tell, Tate's week off is his first that I haven't known about. Either that or his coworkers are protecting him.

Hurried footsteps rush toward me as the elevator door opens, and before I can step inside, I turn around and see Dustin rushing toward me. "You dropped this." He holds his hand out, and I reach for whatever it is, confused about what I might've dropped.

When he hands me a paper clip, my frown deepens.

"He brought his phone in every day," he says, his voice so low I hardly hear it. "Brought it in and left it in his office. I found it on Monday and thought he forgot it, but then he did the same thing on Tuesday, and I brought it to him. He did it again yesterday, so I realized it was probably on purpose and left it alone."

"What are you—"

"You didn't hear it from me." He's backing away before I can ask him to elaborate further. And with that bombshell, he's gone.

CHAPTER SEVEN

TATE

Five Days Before Disappearance

I'm sitting at my desk at work when the email comes in. The article is emailed to me from a bogus, generic email address, and I know enough not to click any links, but the text in the hyperlink catches my eye.

Actually, five words in particular catch my eye.

Bradley Jennings. Dead at 34.

Opening up my search engine, I type in the words. It can't be real, and yet, it is. *What did you do?*

The first search result holds the answers I was searching for. Bradley Jennings, a man I once considered a brother, a man who lived less than half a day's drive away from me and to whom I hadn't spoken more than a few words in nearly twelve years, is dead.

My heart stalls as I skim the article for details and

come up short. The obituary gives a very brief descrip-
tion of the prettier parts of his life but tells nothing of
what must've been a gruesome death. Images of car
crashes flash through my mind, home invasions gone
wrong. It must've been something awful. He was
healthy as far as I knew. Young. He was going to be
getting married soon. According to the obituary, he had
a fiancée and a stepdaughter-to-be. Together, they had
two dogs and a cat. He had a whole life ahead of him, he
was finally figuring it all out, and in a split second, it
was over. Gone, like sand slipping through your fingers.

Life can be so unnecessarily cruel sometimes.

The vibrating of my phone on the desk causes me
to jump, and I nearly fall out of my chair. Checking the
phone screen, I see the familiar words.

Unknown Caller

Before I answer, I hurry across the office and shut
my door. If I ignore him, he'll just call back. I grab the
phone and swipe my thumb across the screen.

"Hello?"

"Did you get it?" His warm, gravelly voice is an
unwelcome intrusion. More than that, it's not the voice
I expected to hear.

"Yes. I saw. Why are you calling me?"

"You know why."

I swallow. "I don't, actually. I was expecting—"

"I'm assuming he called you, too?"

"Yeah," I croak out. "And you?"

"Few days ago, yeah. And now this. What are we going to do about it?"

"What do you mean? It's done, isn't it?"

He breathes in, deep and unsettling. "I wish it were that simple, but no. He was going to tell and now he's gone. That's not a coincidence."

I don't know how to respond. I'm too terrified by what he's insinuating. "I didn't kill him, if that's what you're saying."

"If you didn't and I didn't, there's only one other person who could've. I think it's time we paid him a visit."

CHAPTER EIGHT

CELINE

As I'm driving home from Tate's office, the screen on the car lights up with an incoming call from a number I recognize from my numerous attempts to call it today. I lean forward and tap the green button to answer it.

"Hello?"

"Hi, is this Mrs. Thompson?" The detective's monotonous voice fills the line.

I swallow the lump in my throat, realizing this might be one of the last times I'm called *Mrs.*, but I can't allow myself to think like that. "Um, yes. It is."

"Mrs. Thompson, this is Detective Monroe with the Oakton County Police Department. I received your messages and am sorry it's taken this long to get back with you, but I'm calling you with an update on your husband's case."

My heart stalls as I wait to hear what he's going to

say. *Have they found him? Do they know what happened to him? Did he run away and leave me? Is he hurt? Is he dead?*

I want to ask all of this, but instead, my tongue has turned to cotton, and I can't seem to force my mouth to work at all. Not a sound comes out of my throat, no matter how hard I try.

"We have been able to confirm the identity of the man who was in your husband's vehicle during the crash yesterday," he says.

I take a sharp inhalation of breath. "You have?"

"Does the name Dakota Miller sound familiar to you?"

I rack my brain but come up empty. Finally, thankfully, my voice comes back to me. "No, I don't…I mean, I don't think so."

I can hear him shuffling papers over the line. "Did your husband ever talk about his time at Highland University?"

The question confuses and shocks me in equal measure. "Not…really. It was a long time ago. Why?"

"We've been able to connect your husband with Mr. Miller through their university. We've just spoken to Mr. Miller's next of kin, his wife, who is out of town on a business trip and believed her husband was at work today. When we asked her about your husband or why they might be in contact, why he would be in your husband's vehicle, she couldn't tell us. She said she'd never heard Dakota mention Tate's name, but we did find out that he's also an alumnus of Highland and that he and your husband attended during the same years. It seems that he and your husband were classmates, and though we still can't prove it, between the matching tattoos, the fact that he was in your husband's car with his phone and ID, and the connection to Highland, it's becoming increasingly difficult to deny the likelihood that they knew each other."

I swallow. "What does any of that have to do with why he was driving Tate's car yesterday? Even if they knew each other in college, they weren't still in contact. I'd know if they were. Tate talks to me. He tells me everything." *Almost* everything, apparently. "Did he...I mean, they didn't work together, right? No. I'd know if they did." I answer the question before he has the chance. "Are you any closer to finding Tate? Do you have any new leads aside from this man's name? I'm sorry I've called so much, I just feel like I'm not being told anything. Not that it's your fault, it's just..." I heave a sigh, not bothering to finish the thought. Thankfully, he steps in without waiting.

"Unfortunately, we don't have anything concrete to report just yet, but we're actively following up on a few leads and will be in touch as soon as we can. In the meantime, if you remember anything your husband might've mentioned to you about his time in college, particularly anything that relates to Dakota Miller, please give me a call back at this number so we can discuss it."

"Okay, sure. I will."

"Thank you, Mrs. Thompson. We'll be in touch, okay?"

I nod, though he can't see me, and end the call, my mind spinning. *What in the world was my husband's old college buddy doing driving Tate's car? How did he manage to have a wreck? And where is Tate?*

When I get home, the first thing I do is head to our bedroom and pull out Tate's laptop. His password here is the same as it's always been—our anniversary.

I type it in and unlock the screen, trying to decide where to go first. I open his email account and search for the name the detective gave me: **Dakota Miller.**

To my surprise—it almost feels too easy—there are seventeen results for Dakota Miller in my husband's inbox, spanning back over the last three years, with two of them just before Tate's disappearance.

Most of them are simple and easily explainable—an invitation to an alumni game, a wedding invitation for a classmate.

What's strange is that Tate hasn't replied to a single email from what I can tell, though Dakota kept sending them.

The most recent emails are a bit more confusing. Five days before Tate went missing, Dakota emailed him with a single question mark. Two days before Tate disappeared, he sent an address without an explanation.

Interest piqued, I copy the address and paste it into the internet search bar, but I find that it's the address of an insurance firm a town away. **Nelson Insurance Company.** Could this be related to work somehow? Was that why Dakota and Tate were in touch again? Maybe it is somehow related to the bad appraisal Tate told me about before.

If that was even true.

I hate that it's come to this. That I'm now having to question everything Tate has ever told me. We were never that couple. We trusted each other, had faith in each other. Before the text I confronted him about last week, I can count the number of times I questioned him about anything on less than one hand. He never gave me any reason to doubt him. Or maybe I just saw what I wanted to see. Maybe I didn't look hard enough. *Have I just been foolish all this time?*

I know for certain now that he was lying about more than I knew. That he took a vacation and lied to me about where he was going every day. I feel so stupid. I must *look* so stupid. I rarely questioned anything, and Tate took advantage of that.

I scroll back through his emails and scour each line for anything that might stand out, but there's nothing. Who was this man? Why wasn't Tate responding to him?

If he was simply just an old classmate that Tate had no interest in speaking to, why was he in my husband's car? It's another piece to the puzzle, yet I can't seem to place it. It doesn't seem to fit anywhere inside this mosaic of solutionless clues.

I click on one of the invitations to an alumni game and realize Tate was CC'd to the email with two other guys. It's no surprise to me that I don't recognize either of these names any more than Dakota's. **Aaron Bond and Bradley Jennings.**

Opening up my browser again, I search Aaron's name first.

It takes seconds for the results to load, and when they do, my heart stalls. Aaron Bond works for Nelson Insurance Company. What are the odds this isn't all related somehow?

Without second-guessing myself, I grab my phone and dial the number listed on the website.

"Nelson Insurance, Kristen speaking. How can I help you?"

"Hi, Kristen. I was hoping to speak with Aaron Bond, if he's in."

"Sure," she chirps happily. "Can I tell him who's calling?"

Shoot. I can't be honest here. Somehow, I just know I can't. "Um, Melinda Jones," I say, spouting off the first fake name I can concoct.

"Okay, please hold, Ms. Jones."

Within a few seconds, I hear the trill sound of a phone ringing and then, "Nelson Insurance, thanks for holding. This is Aaron."

"Hi, Aaron." I take a deep breath. "This is Celine Thompson. You don't know me, but I believe you know my husband, Tate—"

"I don't want anything to do with this." His warm tone turns cold in an instant.

"Anything to do with what? I'm sorry, my husband is missing, and I thought—"

"Please don't call here again," he says firmly. "Don't contact me."

"But—"

The line goes dead before I can utter another word. What in the world was that about? Chills line my skin as I think back over the way he spoke to me. Something upset him. *I* upset him, but why? And what did he mean about not wanting anything to do with it?

Hoping I'll have better luck with the second name, I type it into the browser.

Bradley Jennings.

The first result holds answers, just not ones I was hoping for. It's yet another mysterious piece of this unending puzzle. One that just got a lot more serious, too.

Because Bradley Jennings, just like Dakota Miller, and potentially just like Tate, is dead. Stranger still, he died a week ago today.

CHAPTER NINE

TATE

Five Days Before Disappearance

I press my ear to the phone, lowering my voice in the quiet office. "What the hell are you talking about? We're not going to visit Aaron."

Dakota scoffs. "You really don't care what happened to Bradley? You don't want to know?"

"No." I pinch the bridge of my nose between my fingers, leaning forward on my elbows on the desktop. "Because it's not my business anymore. Whatever happened, it's awful, but it's done. Aaron didn't kill him, and you know it."

"I don't know any of you anymore. For all I know, you're the one who killed him."

"For all I know, *you* did," I retort, frustration tingling a muscle in my shoulders. I don't have time for any of this. "Why don't you just call him and ask, like you did me?"

He draws in a long breath. "Well, I tried. You're the one who answered."

My patience is wearing thin as a call comes in from a client. One I can't truly afford to not answer. "Look, I spoke with Aaron last week. He wasn't planning to kill him. He was trying to talk me down from confronting him."

"And did you? Confront him?"

I run my hands through my hair, chewing on the inside of my cheek in frustration. I shouldn't have said that. "No. He called me, and we spoke. I told him he needed to keep his mouth shut, like we agreed."

"And?" Dakota presses.

"And nothing. That's where we left it. I haven't spoken to him since. I had no idea anything had happened to him until I got the obituary. Why'd you send it from some weird address, by the way?" I ask, pulling up the email again and using the mouse to drag the pointer across the phony email address.

"I didn't want it to seem suspicious if I sent it from mine," he says simply, as if that makes any sense at all.

I massage the space between my brows. "Well, it's going to seem a whole lot more suspicious that you created a weird email account to send it. Did you send it from your computer?"

"Um…" He pauses. "Is it bad if I did?"

I drop my head into my hands. "It's all the same IP address, so it's going to be really obvious you created a fake email to send it. So I'm going with yeah, it's really bad."

"Look, whatever. I didn't do anything wrong. All I'm saying is, what are the odds? After all this time, Bradley wants to talk, and days later he's been murdered. Don't tell me you honestly think that's a coincidence. There's no way."

I press my lips together, squeezing my eyes shut as a headache begins to form in my temples. "How do we know anyone killed him? For all we know, he had a car accident or a heart attack."

"Blunt force trauma to the head," Dakota says, stealing my breath with the interruption. "He was found at home alone."

My blood runs cold. "How do you know that? You can't possibly know that."

His voice is emotionless as he responds, sending chills over me. I feel as if I'm going to be sick. "I have a friend who works at the hospital. He was working last night when Bradley was brought in. Said he took something heavy to the back of the head. Doesn't sound like an accident to me."

I squeeze my eyes shut, forcing away the image that fills my head. "That doesn't mean it has anything to do with him contacting us."

He lets out a dry laugh. "It does if he told you what he told me."

"No." My hand balls into a fist. "None of us would've hurt him."

"Someone did. You're awfully sure it wasn't us. Weird you don't care enough to look into it, unless you already know what happened," he says, and I feel as if a cold hand has slipped up the back of my shirt. Every part of me is pure ice.

I inhale sharply, my panic interrupted by another call coming in from the client. "Look, what do you want, Dakota? I'm at work. I need to go."

"No. You need to come with me to meet Aaron. Find out what he knows."

I watch as the call fades from the screen and send a quick text to tell him I'm at a showing and will call him back as soon as possible. "When?"

"Today. Tomorrow. Soon. As soon as we can. We need to talk to him, all of us in one room, until the truth comes out."

I sigh. This is the last thing I need to be doing, but he's right. It's important. We have to know for sure. "Okay, fine. I'll look at my calendar. But then what? Are you really going to accuse him of hurting Bradley? You know the two of them were the closest of any of us."

I hear him release a slow breath. "Then I guess he'll want to find out the truth more than any of us, won't he?"

CHAPTER TEN

CELINE

Bradley Jennings is dead. More notable than that, Bradley Jennings died just six days before Tate disappeared. The thoughts repeat in my head like a broken record determined to drive me mad.

I read through his obituary, but I don't find anything particularly of note. I can't find any news articles about his cause of death either.

Pivoting from one theory to another, I pick up my phone and find my mother-in-law's number in my contacts. She answers quickly, sounding stressed. "Hello? Celine?"

"Daph, I have a question."

"We were just on our way to see you before we head to the police station. Have you heard anything from them? We've been calling all morning, but we're not getting any sort of answers. We just heard back that they want to talk to us about someone Tate went to school with. Do you know what that might be about?"

"Actually, yeah. That's why I'm calling you." It doesn't surprise me in the least to know my in-laws have taken matters into their own hands and are now contacting the police themselves in hopes of getting answers. "They identified the man who was driving Tate's car yesterday. The one who had the wreck."

"They did?" She gasps, and suddenly her voice is farther away, as if she's put me on speakerphone. "Who was it? What did they say? Was he a criminal?"

"He was...actually, he was the person I'm assuming they're going to ask you about, the guy Tate went to school with. I was hoping you might know more about him than I do. I couldn't tell them anything."

"Well, what's his name?" Lane asks.

"Dakota Miller. Tate never mentioned him to me, but apparently they went to Highland together. Do you happen to remember him?"

There's an eerie silence on the other line, and then I hear my mother-in-law inhale. "Dakota Miller? You're sure that's who they said?"

"Yes." They must know him.

"They were friends," Lane says finally with a shaky breath. "Best friends. Brothers, practically, and they took a lot of the same classes. We haven't heard that name in years."

"He was the boy who died yesterday?" Daph says, sounding as if she's on the verge of tears. "You're absolutely positive? It doesn't make any sense. That can't be true."

"We're pulling into your subdivision now," Lane says. "Let us get into the house, and we can talk about it more."

"Yeah, okay." I end the call and go and wait by the door as they pull into the driveway. They get out of their car slowly, deep in discussion with haunted looks in their eyes. When they reach the doorway, Daph pulls me into a tight hug, sobs tearing through her.

"I can't believe this," she whispers. "I just can't believe it."

I hug her back just as tightly, though my own tears seem to have dried up at the source. I can't bring myself to cry or even, truthfully, to feel sad for this man, when I have to be suspicious of him instead. Why did he have our car? Why did he wreck it? *Where is my husband?*

"Okay, so"—she smooths her hands over my hair, her bright blue, tear-filled eyes darting back and forth between mine—"what exactly did they tell you about Dakota? Are they certain it's him?"

"I guess so. They asked if I knew him, and I said no. And they said they'd confirmed that they went to school together, and Dakota was the one driving the car. I went through Tate's email, and there were just a few messages between them, or from Dakota to Tate, more like."

"Messages? Tate hasn't mentioned that they've been

in touch." Daph shakes her head, twisting her lips in thought.

"I think it was all just boring stuff—invitations to alumni events, mostly. And one address that he sent a few days ago, but it was to an insurance office out in Dublin, so I think it might've been work-related. The police were already at Tate's office yesterday evening, so if that's the case, maybe that's how they connected the dots and figured out who Dakota was." I pause, thinking. "Do you know what happened to cause them to stop talking?"

"Oh, I don't think anything happened. They just grew apart after college, went their separate ways. You know how it goes. You promise to keep in touch, and then life gets in the way." Daphne looks down, dabbing her eyes with her fingers. "Those boys were inseparable in college. I just can't believe he's gone." She sniffles as Lane tucks an arm around her. "They were more than friends. They were brothers. They were, I mean, they practically lived at our house. They were such good boys."

"What about Bradley Jennings or Aaron Bond?" I ask, probably pushing my luck.

Her eyes widen slightly. "Are they involved in this, too?"

"Do you know them?"

She nods, but slowly, hesitantly. "They were all boys in school together. But Tate hasn't spoken to or about them in years, as far as I know." She looks to Lane, who nods in agreement.

"They were almost always included on the email threads between Dakota and Tate, but no one had responded as far as I could see. When I looked them up, I learned that Bradley, um, he also passed away recently. I'm so sorry, Daphne."

Tears fill her eyes and overflow down her cheeks as she stares at me, her chin trembling. "Both of them? Bradley and Dakota are gone? You're sure? And now Tate's missing? It doesn't make sense." She wraps her arms around herself, leaning into Lane, who holds her against his side, looking away from me.

The weight of their grief is palpable, swelling to fill the room.

"I'm so sorry. I couldn't find a lot of information, but it seems like a strange coincidence. The other man on the email list was named Aaron Bond—"

She winces, bracing herself. "Oh, tell me Aaron isn't—"

"He's still alive," I assure her, easing her panic only slightly. "But he wouldn't talk to me."

"You reached out to him?" Lane asks, meeting my eyes for the first time since I delivered the news. His arm is still rubbing up and down over Daphne's back.

"I called his office phone. I thought he might be able to help, if he knew Tate, but he hung up on me."

"Well, that isn't like him," Daphne says, staring off

into space. "Maybe we could reach out to him since he knows us." She looks at Lane, who frowns.

"Knew us practically a decade ago. Besides, I don't see what good it'll do," Lane says, twisting his lips in thought, arms crossed.

"It'll be the whole group...gone," Daphne says, her tone somber. "If anything happens to Aaron. If someone is targeting the boys for some reason."

"Targeting them? Why would you say that?" Lane stares at her as if she's lost her mind, but I'm not sure she's wrong.

She presses her lips together. "What else could it mean? The whole group gone so close together?"

"You keep saying that. What do you mean, the whole group?" I ask.

She pauses, staring at me as if she's trying to decide what to say. "All of Tate's friends from college. Dakota, Bradley, now Tate. That doesn't seem like a coincidence."

"That was all of his friends?"

She nods.

"Now don't be getting any kind of conspiracy theory in your head, Daph," Lane says, his voice skeptical. My father-in-law deals in the world of numbers and facts, so it doesn't surprise me in the least that he's dismissing what Daphne is saying, but she's thinking along the same lines I have been. It can't be just a coincidence, even more so with what I've just learned. "These boys haven't been in contact in years. What reason would anyone have to target them? You said it yourself…they were good boys."

"Would you mind calling him?" I ask. "I think you're right. If he knew you, he might be more willing to talk to you than he was me."

Daphne's eyes widen as she looks at Lane, then back at me. "I don't see how it could hurt, but I don't have his number anymore. Do you want me to try the office phone you called earlier?"

I nod, retrieving my phone from my pocket and rattling the number off to her. Pressing send, she places the phone to her ear and waits.

After a few moments, her face lights up. "Yes, hello. I'm hoping to speak with Aaron Bond, please."

She pauses.

"You can tell him it's Daphne Thompson."

My throat goes dry, and I suddenly wish she hadn't given him her real name. There's another long pause and then her face falls. "Oh. No, of course. Yes, just have him call me back. Please tell him it's urgent." She gives her number to the receptionist before ending the call, looking as defeated as I feel. "She said he was on a call."

I don't need to say it. Somehow, I know we all feel it. Aaron Bond isn't going to take our calls. He's ignoring us, and I need to know why.

Daphne looks up at Lane, her chin quivering. His eyes dance between hers, their broken expressions cracking the last of my resolve. Before anyone can say anything, she begins to weep.

"I just want him home," she sobs. "I just want my son home."

He pulls her into his chest as tears tickle the back of my throat, and I step away. Lane was probably right with what he said earlier. Going down rabbit holes isn't helping anyone right now. We have to deal with what we know for certain. And what I know for certain is that Aaron is potentially one of the only members of the friend group left, and he's also the one avoiding us right now.

I need to fix that. Chase this rabbit. But I need to do it alone.

"Hey, guys, I'm really sorry to do this, but I have somewhere to be." I pat my mother-in-law's arm. "I was just on my way out when you caught me, but feel free to stay here. Mom will be by with the boys after school, and I should be back within a few hours."

"Do you want us to go with you?" Lane asks.

"I'm okay. I just have an errand to run."

"We were on our way to the police station anyway," Daphne reminds us both, drying her eyes. "And once we're there, I'm going to give them a piece of my mind. They should be doing more than what they are. A search party. Something. If your errand can wait, you can come with us."

I wince. "I can't." This feels too important, but I can't say that. "But tell me what they say, okay? Please?"

I can tell I've upset Daphne by the way her mouth tenses. She's ordinarily such an easygoing, kind mother-in-law, but I know I'm failing her right now. Still, I have my own investigation to do, and they have theirs. This path feels right to me.

Together, we make our way back out the door, and I lock it behind us before giving them both a hug and settling into my car. I have an email from our car insurance agent, so I start to call him back, but I stop when I spot an incoming call from another blocked number.

This time, I nearly don't answer, but how can I not when it could be Tate?

"Hello?" I watch my in-laws backing out of the driveway before I put my car in reverse.

Like last time, I'm met with only silence, but unlike last time, I'm more angry than hopeful.

"Who is this?" I demand.

Nothing. No response. No breathing. For all I know, this is a robocall.

"Tate, is that you?"

Nothing. Rage bubbles in my belly.

"Or maybe it's you, Aaron?"

Something shifts in the air as I wonder if I'm right. Before I have time to ponder too long, I hear a breath. A single puff of air, like a sigh released, and then the call ends.

CHAPTER ELEVEN

TATE

Two Days Before Disappearance

Nelson Insurance Company is a shithole.

I'm not just saying it because I'm pissed I have to be here right now, either. The place looks as if it's ready to cave in. The yellow stone building is turning green and needs to be power washed. The parking lot has no painted white lines and is cracking in every direction.

The place is a mess, in short, and I can't get out of here soon enough. When the brown truck pulls into the parking lot, I recognize Dakota at once. He has the same dark-brown hair—a shade or two darker than mine—and the same haircut and stocky build that he's always had. It's been nearly a decade since I saw him last, but it feels like no time has passed. Not nearly enough time, anyway.

My old friends always bring a side of myself out

that I don't like. I slip out of my car and cross the parking lot, kicking a soda can with a fading label out of my way as I go.

"Tate." Dakota holds out his hand, and I shake it. It feels oddly formal, but then again, we're practically strangers. Dakota's tried to reach out a few times over the years, but we all ignored him. He was always the one who couldn't let the past go while the rest of us were so desperate to forget.

"Let's get this over with," I say with a groan, jutting my head toward the building where Aaron works. "You're sure he's here?"

"I set up a meeting with him this morning." Dakota tucks his hands into the pockets of his slacks.

"You mean he actually took it?"

"Well, I didn't give my real name." He scoffs, looking at me as if the question was dumb. Truth be told, I guess it was. If Dakota was the type to hold on, Aaron was the type to let go. To run away, even more than I did. Everything that happened back then changed him in a way I can't explain.

Then again, it changed us all.

"Right." I grab the door and pull it open. The place is small and feels more like a car dealership than an insurance office. I can't imagine the type of person who'd trust this company with their money.

At the sound of the bell above the door, I hear a set of footsteps walking our way from inside one of the three offices. As Aaron comes into view, I see the moment he realizes what's happening crossing his face as the smile fades to a scowl. The skin around his eyes smooths out, his lips forming a frown. His usually warm brown eyes go stony.

"What are you two doing here?" he asks, leaning his head back a bit, clearly not pleased to see us.

"Came to pay you a visit," Dakota says, always cocky as shit.

"I'm working." Aaron scowls. "You shouldn't be here. I've got nothing to say to you." He glances up at a camera on the wall that I assume is more for looks than actual security.

"Come on, man. We just want to chat. We'll be out of here in a few minutes." I'm actively trying to charm him, as if he's a client, but to my surprise, it seems like it might be working.

"What do you want?"

I lower my voice. "We should go somewhere a bit more private, don't you think?"

"Fine." He turns, waving for us to follow him, and once we're in his office, he shuts the door. "I have a meeting in a few minutes, so—"

"No, you don't," Dakota says. "I have you fully booked for the next forty-five minutes. Nice to meet you. I'm Carter Wellington the Third." He looks proud of himself.

It takes Aaron a moment to process, and then he scowls, refusing the hand Dakota's holding out. "Oh, you ass."

"I thought the pompous name was a nice touch, didn't you?"

Aaron sits down, not bothering to tell us we should do the same, but we do anyway. "Alright, let's just get right to it, okay? I have work to do. What do you want?"

"We're here about Bradley," Dakota says plainly, folding his hands on top of the desk.

Aaron's face pales.

"I take it you heard," I say.

He nods slowly, visibly shaken. "Yeah. Yeah, of course I heard."

"Had you talked to him or seen him that day?" Dakota asks.

Aaron swallows. "Why? Had you?"

"You had." Dakota leans forward, sounding as shocked as I feel. This was just the warm-up to the conversation. We didn't actually think he'd talked to Bradley that day any more than we'd talked to him. "What did he say?"

Aaron's eyes shift between the two of us, then down to his hands. "We didn't talk that day, but we talked a lot in the days…before."

"Were you two still in touch?'" I ask. "Before all of this, I mean.

"Look." Aaron sighs. "What do you want? Why are you here? Whatever it is, just spit it out. I haven't heard from you in twelve years, so I know damn well this isn't a social call."

"We want to know what happened to Bradley," I say firmly.

"And you think I would know?"

"Well"—Dakota leans back in his chair—"put it this way: we *don't* think you *don't* know."

He purses his lips. "I had nothing to do with his death, okay? I haven't seen or spoken to the guy in years, until he called me. Like he called all the rest of you. He told me the same thing he told all of us."

"Which was?" Dakota asks.

"He was getting married, obviously," Aaron says. "This fall. You know this."

"I want to hear it from you," Dakota says.

Aaron pinches his lips between his fingers as Dakota taps his knuckles on the arm of the chair.

"He was getting married, and he wanted to tell her the truth about what happened back then. He wanted our blessing. He said he was going to call all of you, but he reached out to me first."

When Bradley had said those words to me, it was like an ice-cold blow to the stomach. Even now, I feel the chill hearing them spoken out loud.

Dakota's face curls into a sneer that isn't unlike the one I feel building on my own face.

"I guess he thought mine would be the easiest to get first, and that I'd help convince you two," Aaron says.

"And what did you tell him?" I ask.

Aaron stares at me for a second too long, and I raise my brows, urging him to answer. "I told him under no circumstances did I think he should tell anyone what happened that night. We swore that we wouldn't, we made a pact, and we have to keep our word." Aaron nods, glancing down at his hands. "We were brothers first, no matter what. We have to protect each other."

"I told him the same thing," I say. "When he called me. How did he take it when you told him?"

"I don't know. He seemed convinced, I guess, but I couldn't tell. He was in love. Stupid. He wanted her to know everything before they got married."

"Do you think he told her?" I ask again, worry flooding me.

"I don't know."

"Well, what *do* you know?" I shout, my words dripping with venom. Panic is flooding my veins, and I feel as if I can't catch my breath.

"Come on, man, ease up. I'm telling you everything," Aaron says, hands up in surrender.

"If the truth about that night ever got out, my life would be ruined," I remind him in a bitter whisper.

"And ours wouldn't?" he asks, his auburn brows rising to meet his receding hairline and buzz cut. "We're in this together."

I press my tongue to the roof of my mouth, weighing my next words. "We've never been together in this. Not really. You know it wouldn't affect you two the same way it would me. I have a hell of a lot more to lose if the truth comes out."

"We were there, too. It affects us just as much as it

does you, and the truth about it ever coming out would be equally damning for every one of us," he says firmly. "And that's all I know. I told him to keep his mouth shut, advised him not to talk to you, which we know he didn't listen to, and that was that. We didn't speak again after that, and next thing I knew, I was reading his obituary. To be completely honest—" He cuts himself off.

"What?" I ask, leaning in. "Say it."

He braces himself, slowing his words. "To be... completely honest, I worried he wasn't going to listen, that he was going to tell, and you guys couldn't stop him so you—" He cuts himself off again, tilting his head from side to side.

"Killed him?" Dakota says. "I said the same thing. Someone in this room has the most to gain from him being dead."

His eyes find mine, and I pin him with a glare. "I didn't kill him."

"Me either," Aaron agrees.

"Same," Dakota says. "So we need to find out who did."

Later, when we're leaving with more questions than answers, Dakota says, "We need to find the fiancée. Find out what she knows."

"I don't have time for this," I say, shaking my head.

"Do you have time for jail, then? Because if he told her—"

"If he told her, what? What are we going to do?" I

demand. "Take her out? Kill her? Are you really suggesting we—"

"I'm just suggesting..." He holds up a hand, speaking slowly. "We *advise* her to keep quiet. That's all."

"Threaten her?" I scoff. "No. I have to work. I can't go track down our friend's grieving widow. Sorry." I turn to walk away from him, but his next words stop me in my tracks.

"You were right in there. If all of this goes south, it's you who will take the fall for all of it. We were accessories, sure, but it's your life that blows up. Not mine. You think your pretty little wife will stay with you if she knows the truth about who you are? What you did?"

I spin around so fast it startles him, my hand balled into a fist. "Don't threaten me."

His hands go up in surrender, but his expression is cocky, not scared. "Wouldn't dream of it. I'm merely trying to help, *boss.*" He winks.

I groan, scrubbing my hand over my face. "I have to work," I repeat.

"So take some time off."

"How much time?"

"A week," he says. "Take the rest of the week off, like you did today, and let's get some things handled, then you can be back to your cushy little life in no time."

CHAPTER TWELVE

CELINE

Nelson Insurance is two hours from our house, in a tiny building between a gas station and a liquor store. It's older with paint that needs updating and a logo decal on the door that is missing two letters.

I have no idea what to expect once I get in there. Will they just let me see Aaron? Will he already be with someone? Will he even be in the office, or does he work from home most days?

I know, once he realizes who I am, that he'll send me away. I'm just hoping I can appeal to him as a person before he does. If he was friends with Tate before, surely there's some shred of humanity in him that will want to help me.

I cross the parking lot, stepping over cracks in the pavement with thick tufts of grass growing up through them.

As I walk inside, I'm hit with a wave of stale air, the

ching-ching of the bell above the door, and the loud hum of the air conditioning unit. There's no receptionist at the desk like there usually is at Tate's office, but after a few moments, I hear someone making their way toward the front.

A shorter, balding man with a serious face and a coffee stain on the belly of his white shirt walks out of an office, tugging at the waist of his pants. "Well, hello there. I thought I heard someone come in." He holds out his hand with a warm smile. "Sorry about the wait. Kristen's out to lunch, but I'm Aaron. One of the insurance agents here. Can I help you with something today?"

"Actually, yes." I brace myself for the worst. "Is there any way we could speak in your office?"

He hesitates, and I worry I've blown my cover, but eventually, he says, "Sure. I'm sorry, I didn't get your name."

I consider lying, but eventually decide against it. "Celine."

"Nice to meet you, Celine." He steps back, still appearing wary, and leads me toward an office in the back. The office is generic, with old furniture and cheap, gray carpet. There are a few photographs on a lateral filing cabinet behind his desk, and my eyes immediately drift to one of him fishing off a boat, shirtless and turned away from the camera. His shoulder boasts the same tattoo Tate's does. The same tattoo that Dakota's had also.

"Now, then. What can I do for you?" He sits down in his chair and rolls it up to his desk, studying me with his hands folded under his chin.

I take a deep breath. "My husband is Tate Thompson."

His body tenses, but I rush to continue.

"Please don't send me away. I know you didn't want to talk to me over the phone, but I've come all this way and I just need your help. I think you're the only one who can help me."

"I can't help you," he says firmly, shaking his head. "I'm sorry. I wish I could, but I can't."

"My mother-in-law, Daphne, she spoke highly of you. Said you were all friends in college. She told me you were a good person, that you *are* a good person."

He sighs, resting his forehead against his knuckles as he stares down at the desktop. "That was a long time ago. I hadn't spoken to Tate in years. Mrs. Thompson is very kind, but she doesn't know me anymore. And neither does Tate."

"He had your office's physical address in his email, sent from Dakota Miller, who I believe was also your friend."

He looks up at me with an exhausted expression that I feel in my bones. "I don't know anything about that. Like I told you on the phone, I don't want anything to do with whatever this is."

"All of your friends are dead or missing," I say, getting straight to the point. "And I think you know why. If they were truly your friends, surely you would want to help find Tate, to bring him home safely."

He shakes his head. "I wish I did. I wish I could help you. Tate was a good guy."

"*Was?*" I say, my nose scrunched in disgust. "He's not dead."

He pinches his lips together. "Look, you should go. I'm sorry I can't be of more help, but I don't know what's going on, and I don't have any business getting involved."

"Why was Nelson Insurance's address in his email? Can you at least tell me that? Did he come here? Were you guys working together on something?"

"No. I have no idea why Dakota would've sent him the address." He stands. "Maybe they were going to send me a card."

"You all have that same tattoo." I gesture toward the picture, then touch the back of my shoulder, where the same tattoo would fit on my skin if I had it. "The lion. What does it mean? Tate never told me."

He looks at the photo, scowling. "It was stupid college stuff. We were drunk and thought they looked cool." He holds out his arm, gesturing toward the door. "Please don't make me call the cops. This is my place of business. You can't just show up." His shoulders rise with a heavy breath. "Please just don't come here again, okay? I hope you find Tate, but there's nothing else I can do to help you. I've left that period of my life in the past, and that's where I want it to stay."

I nod, gathering my purse and standing, but think better of it and grab a sticky note and pen, jotting down my phone number. "Please, just...if you think of anything, please call me."

He nods but looks annoyed, and finally, I leave with nothing more than I arrived with. When I make it to the car, I realize the small silver lining is that thought is not entirely true. One thing that came from this trip is that I now know the tattoos were a thing among friends in college, and that they all had them, not just Tate and Dakota. Whether or not that means anything, I'm not sure, but it's a piece of information I didn't have before, and I'll take it.

As I drive across town, I run through the conversation in my head. I don't know why he doesn't want to help if Tate was ever truly his friend, but I can see not wanting to get involved in an active investigation, especially if they haven't spoken in years. Still, if they were truly as close as brothers like Daphne and Lane described, I can't imagine not wanting to answer questions or help if there was a way I could. I think about the girls I was close with in high school—women I haven't spoken with in years. If something were to happen to them, even if I knew nothing, I'd want to be involved. I'd want to help. Unless he's hiding something, the way Aaron is acting doesn't make any sense to me.

I just wish I knew why Dakota sent him Aaron's

work address a few days ago. It has to mean something, doesn't it?

When I pull into my driveway, all thoughts of Aaron and our conversation are wiped away by the sight of a police car waiting for me.

I step out of the car at the same time Detective Monroe does. Moments later, my mom pops her head out of the house. I wave at her cautiously. I can't tell if she looks worried or upset from where I'm standing, and I hate that.

The detective walks toward me. "Afternoon, Mrs. Thompson. Sorry to pop in unannounced."

"Oh, um, no problem. Have you been waiting long?"

"Not at all. Just got here, and your mom informed me you'd be home any minute. I was just getting ready to try to call you."

I glance back at the car. "Oh. Is everything alright? Did something happen?"

"I just wanted to follow up with you about something we came across during our investigation." He folds his hands in front of his stomach, widening his stance, and my stomach drops.

Whatever it is, it requires more than a phone call. This must be serious. I swallow. "Okay."

He reaches into his jacket pocket and pulls out a notepad, flipping it open. "Mrs. Thompson, what can you tell me about the large withdrawal from your investment account on the day before your husband disappeared?"

"My…" My heart stalls. "My what?"

"The joint investment account that you share with your husband as part of a mutual fund. Do you know what I'm referring to? It looks like it had a balance of around two hundred and sixty-four thousand dollars in it."

I nod. "I know which one you're talking about, yes, but I don't know anything about a withdrawal. How much is missing?"

He looks down at his paper again quickly and closes the notebook. "All of it, Mrs. Thompson. Every cent."

CHAPTER THIRTEEN

TATE

One Day Before Disappearance

I don't like lying to Celine, but at this point, what choice do I have? Everything could be falling apart at the seams, shredding the carefully placed pieces of my life, if I don't figure out what happened to Bradley or at least make sure he never told anyone what we did.

I don't know, maybe Dakota has gotten in my head. Maybe I'm just paranoid, but if there's even the slightest chance that Bradley told his fiancée about what we did—or anyone else for that matter—I have to know and then decide how to handle it. I just don't know yet what that means.

I'm not sure what I'm willing to do to keep our secret—to keep my life intact—anymore. I'm not the person I was back then.

I'm making my way out of the office when I hear Dustin calling my name. I spin around to find him chasing me, and my heart sinks. He's holding my phone in his hand, a bright smile beaming on his face. "Don't want to forget this," he sings. "It was lying on your desk."

"Oh, shoot. Right. Thanks. I must've…forgotten it." *Well, this works out great, doesn't it? Absolutely perfect.*

His smile falters just a hair, and I can't help wondering if he suspects I'm lying, so I grin wider, tucking my phone into my pocket and patting it. "I'll, uh, I'll see you around, okay?"

"Have fun with all those projects," he teases, zipping back inside.

I make my way to the car door, cursing my luck. I can't take the phone back inside now, and I also can't take it with me out of town. I could tell Celine I was meeting a client, I guess, but I don't deal with properties two hours outside of the city, so I'm not sure she would believe it. I could say I'm meeting a client who lives outside of the city but owns a property or is looking for a property here. It wouldn't be the most illogical thing, but I also can't risk her starting to make connections between Nelson Insurance and me. It's just too big of a gamble.

If I turn my phone off, my trusting wife will become suspicious. At least, I know I would be if the roles were reversed. I could call a cab, I guess, and leave my phone in the car, but the charge to get hours away and back would be astronomical. So I do the only thing I can think to do at this moment.

Dakota picks up quickly as if he were expecting my call.

"I need you to pick me up."

"When? *Now?* Why?"

"Yes, now. I did what you said. I took the week off, and I'm going to talk to Bradley's fiancée. But I need to leave my phone at the office so my wife doesn't know where I'm going, which means I need to leave it in my car. Which means I need another car to get me to Dublin."

"You were going to go without me?" he asks.

"Didn't really feel like a two-man job."

"Got it," he says, sounding slightly offended but clearly trying to hide it. "Well, I'm not in town right now, so it'll take me like thirty or so minutes to get there, but I'll be there as soon as I can."

"Cool. Thanks. See ya." I end the call and tuck my phone into the glovebox, checking my reflection in the car mirror. I'm exhausted and it shows, but I've always been good at putting on the bravest of faces.

True to his word, Dakota shows up less than an hour later, rolling his truck up right next to where I'm parked. I slip out of my car and into the truck quickly, shutting the door before muttering, "Thanks again."

"When I didn't hear from you yesterday, I was starting to think you were going to ignore me."

I was, but I'm not going to admit that now. "I just needed some time to get a game plan figured out."

"And what is the game plan?" He pulls out of the parking lot, glancing over at me. "Obviously for you to go to Dublin alone."

Ignoring his apparent attempt at wit, I buckle in. "We're going to Dublin to check on his fiancée and see what she'll tell us about his death."

I can't tell if he's on the verge of laughing or screaming at me. "That's it? That's your plan? We just stop at the house of a woman we've never met, who doesn't know us from Adam, and say, 'Hey, give us the scoop on the dead guy you almost married'?"

I scowl. "Well, obviously not like that. I figure we can stop and pick up some flowers on the way." I pat the pocket where I've stored a bit of cash. "Tell her we are old friends of Bradley's and we're sorry to hear about his death. Just sort of get a feel for things. Play it by ear. If we find out he's told her about that night, we'll tell her it's a lie. That Bradley was always a little off." I feel disgusting even saying it, lying like this, but I have no real choice. I made my decision back then, a decision I've regretted every day since I made it, and I can't go back on it now. I can only accept the consequences of what I've done and try to move forward and be better. "We'll offer to help her however we can."

Dakota nods and shifts his gaze as we stop at a red light. When he speaks again, he's looking directly ahead. "I need to tell you something."

I wait.

He clears his throat, rubbing a hand across his mouth. "I'm starting to think..." He pauses, licking his lips. "What if we've been wrong about all of this? What if the person who killed Bradley actually wasn't any of us? What if it was someone else entirely? Someone who knows what we did and wants to get revenge or force us to confess or something?"

"What?" I cock my head to the side, studying him. "Do you mean his fiancée?"

"Possibly. Just someone that's not any of us. Someone who found out, either back then or more recently."

"Why would you think that? Why would anyone who knew back then have waited this long to do something about it? And if they just found out, that means one of us talked. Did you tell someone?"

"No," he says, his voice steady. "No, of course not. I'm not stupid. We said we wouldn't tell a soul, and I haven't. Not even Tosha. We've been married three years, and I haven't brought it up once. I wouldn't do that to you guys or myself." He pauses. "Why? Did you?"

"You know I haven't. You said it yourself, I have the most to lose."

"Not even when you were drunk or something?"

"I don't drink." My brows draw together. "This is getting oddly specific, and now I feel like you definitely told someone."

"No." He cuts a line through the air with his hand. "I didn't, but I've just been wondering lately because I'm starting to think I'm being followed."

I cut a glance over my shoulder, checking out the back window. "What are you talking about?"

"No. Not right now," Dakota says. "At home. At the store. On my way home from work. It's always the same black car. A Lexus, I think. I just keep seeing it. They're following me. Watching me. What if they did the same thing to Bradley before—" He cuts his words off, nodding with wide eyes. "What if they're coming after me next?"

"Well, you should've mentioned all of this before you agreed to drive me to Dublin, don't you think?" I check over my shoulder again.

"I want answers as much as you do," he says. "Besides, I haven't seen it yet today. They usually follow me home after work."

"Why didn't you mention it before now?"

"Would you have believed me?" he snarls with disbelief. He's not wrong. I don't know if I believe him even now. "There's more," he adds after a few minutes.

Unbelievable. "Of course there is. What else could there be?"

"Last night, when I got home from work, there was a burned book lying on my welcome mat with a note that said, 'Shhh.'"

"A burned book?" My brows draw down. "Seriously?"

He nods, twisting his lips. "Look, believe me, I know it sounds crazy, but it was there. How else do you explain that?"

"What book was it?"

He cuts a glance my way, and something in my gut flips. "That's the worst part. It was *The Catcher in the Rye.* Which would mean absolutely nothing to me, except..." He doesn't go on, doesn't need to. The second he said the title, my entire body went rigid. We both know what that book means, and only someone who knows about that night would understand its significance. "Even if I could write everything else off—being followed, Bradley's death—there's absolutely no way that book being on my doorstep is anything but a sign that someone knows, especially with a note that all but tells me to keep my mouth shut. Or..." He scratches his head. "Maybe they meant *shhh* as more of, like, a tease. Because of the secret. Because we kept it quiet. I don't know. I don't think it's a coincidence. Whether it's someone who wants us to stay quiet or someone who wants what we did back then to come out, I'm not sure. But I think they're targeting us all. And I think I'm next."

I turn to look out the window, trying to process everything he's telling me. "I don't know, man. It seems far-fetched."

"More far-fetched than our friend being murdered?"

"We still don't know that he was murdered. Just that he had a head injury. Maybe he fell."

"Sure," he says, sounding defeated. "Maybe."

"Look, I'm not saying you're wrong, just that I hope you're not right. It's like I said earlier, I can't make it make sense in my head. If they knew what we did back then—enough to know the detail about *The Catcher in the Rye*—why would they have waited this long to come after us?"

"Unless they just found out. Like if Bradley's guilty conscience led to him telling a friend or a therapist, if not his fiancée."

"Even if he did, how would they have known to track us down? Why would they be following you instead of just reporting it all to the police? And why not me? I'm the one who killed—" I cut myself off, refusing to replay that night ever again. "I'm the one they should target. The guilty one."

He doesn't agree, but I doubt he disagrees either. "What other possible solution is there, though? What else could that book mean? Give me one viable, plausible theory, and I will latch onto it like a life preserver."

I rack my brain for one, a single idea that makes sense as to why that specific book, or any book for that matter would be burned and placed on his doorstep. But there are no explanations that make sense, so I say nothing.

We make the rest of the drive out to Dublin mostly in silence, both seemingly lost in our own thoughts. It's strange. I once knew everything there was to know about this person sitting beside me. I knew his fears, his goals, the girls he liked, the music he was into, the movies he hated. Now he's practically a stranger. I don't even know where he works. We went through something so terrible and formative, and it forever changed us. We can't go back to being the boys who were friends. The scar from that night is permanent and disfiguring, forever a stain on who we were. Try as we might, neither of us can escape it.

We stop at a grocery store a few miles from Bradley's home address and grab a bouquet of flowers. Celine prefers tulips, though she'd rather have chocolates than flowers any day of the week, but I have no idea if this woman likes flowers or has a preference for which ones we pick up.

I'm sure her house is filled with flowers from the funeral at the moment. Still, it feels wrong to show up empty-handed.

With the flowers in hand, we arrive at the address Bradley had listed in the school's alumni directory. It's a quaint blue house with black shutters. One story with a large porch spanning the length of the house.

It fits somehow. I can picture him here. Safe. Building a life. If Bradley were a house, he would be this one. Ordinary but comfortable. Welcoming.

That makes losing him so much harder. I have no right to grieve for him. I had been out of his life for more than a decade. I don't get to be sad or miss him when I made no effort to fix it when he was alive. I know that, and still...I do. I can't help thinking of who he was. How different I wish things had been.

We approach the house in silence and knock on the door, and I have to wonder if Dakota is thinking the same things. He gets to grieve if he wants. He tried, maybe even more than I saw. He sent emails. He texted. He *tried*.

He's the only one of us who did.

Within a few moments, a woman answers. She has long, black hair and green eyes, bloodshot from crying or lack of sleep—or both.

"Can I help you?" she asks before we can introduce ourselves.

"Are you Andrea?" I ask, recalling the name Bradley had attached to his Facebook relationship status and in his obituary.

She nods, crossing her arms and keeping the screened door shut between us.

"We're old friends of Bradley's. We went to school together. I'm Tate, and this is Dakota." I watch for a hint of recognition in her eyes, but there is none. "We were so sorry to hear about him passing."

"We wanted to come to the funeral, but we didn't hear about it in time," Dakota adds. "We're a few hours away. I live in Groff Park and Tate's outside of Dale."

She nods slowly but still doesn't open the door.

"Anyway, we can just leave these here, if you want.

We're sorry to have bothered you. We wanted to give our condolences in person." I move to set the flowers down, and she slowly opens the door, stopping me.

"Were you still in contact with Bradley?" she asks, her quiet voice trembling.

"I wish I could say yes, but the truth is we'd lost touch. We hadn't spoken in years," I admit. "But we were very close in college. I wish we hadn't let it go so long."

"He never mentioned you. He didn't really talk too much about his past," she says, studying me. Her eyes dance over my features slowly. My face burns under the intense scrutiny. "But...he has photos of him and his friends from college. I think I recognize you from some of them."

I give a soft smile and scratch the back of my neck. "Yeah, probably. We were pretty much together all the time. Same sports and clubs. He was roommates with our other friend, Aaron. We'd hoped he could come, but he couldn't get the time off of work."

She holds her hand out finally, taking the flowers from me. "Well, thank you. It was kind of you to come. Really. You didn't have to."

"Oh. It's the least we could do," Dakota says. "Bradley would've done the same for us."

She smiles softly but doesn't respond.

"I...I hate to ask this," I say, "but...can I ask how he died? Was he sick or..." My heart races in my chest as I wait for the answer, or for her to tell me it's none of my business.

"The police think it was a robbery gone wrong." Her voice cracks, and her tired eyes line with tears. "He was here. My daughter had a dance competition in Savannah, and I'd taken her, so we didn't get home until late. We came home and found him in the kitchen. He'd been..." She touches a hand to the back of her head gingerly, eyes staring—remembering—in horror. Without finishing, she clears her throat and blinks away fresh tears. "There were no signs of forced entry, but we left the doors unlocked all the time."

"Was there anything taken?" I ask.

She shakes her head. "No. Nothing we could find, anyway. We don't have a lot of money. I don't understand what they were looking for, but whatever it was couldn't have been worth his life. There's nothing here worth dying over. He would've just given it to them." Her voice cracks again, and she covers her mouth. "I'm sorry."

I shake my head. "No. *I'm* so sorry." My hand goes out toward her as if I'm going to touch her arm, but I think better of it and pull my hand back as I picture what she said. "Do you...do you have security footage? Any way to have seen who it was?"

"No." She sniffles, wiping her nose. "We've never had any trouble. It's a quiet neighborhood, and we just never thought it would happen to us." With a dry, regretful breath, she adds, "God, how naive does that sound?"

I nod, assuming as much, but I had to ask. "It's not your fault. I'm just so sorry he's gone. Is there anything we can do? Anything we can help with or get for you?"

She shakes her head, still not opening the door all the way. She doesn't trust us completely, and I can't say I blame her. "No, thank you. We'll be okay. He'd want us to be okay."

"Bradley was a good guy. He really loved you."

Her brows quirk down. "I thought you said you hadn't spoken."

"He must've." I amend my words. "He always said he'd never get married, but from the pictures in the obituary, I've never seen him look so happy."

She smiles, but it doesn't reach her eyes as we say goodbye and head for the truck.

"What do you think?" Dakota asks once we're inside.

"Well, I don't think she knows anything."

His lips pinch together. "I don't know. I don't trust her."

The words aren't shocking, but I don't know what to do with them, so I say nothing as we pull down the drive and away from the house of the brother we'll never see again, the brother we failed.

CHAPTER FOURTEEN

CELINE

"I don't understand. What do you mean everything is gone?" I stare at the detective, hoping with all hope that this is some sort of prank.

Tate convinced me to put our money into an investment account rather than a traditional 401k years ago because he said it would be easier to get to it if we ever needed it. But he wouldn't have stolen it from us, would he? He wouldn't have taken all our savings, the nest egg we built for the boys' futures, without telling me. I have to believe that, but the longer I hold onto the version of my husband I thought I knew, the more and more I look and feel like a fool.

"The day before your husband disappeared, there was a withdrawal of the full amount made."

My voice is breathless. "I don't...I mean...how could he...where did it go? Where is the money?"

"We're trying to figure that out right now, and we

should have the answers within the next day or so, but I was hoping you could help us without waiting for the paper trail to turn up."

"I have no idea. Tate never said anything. I wouldn't…I mean, he wouldn't…" I gather my composure, stilling the shake in my voice. "He never mentioned taking any money out of our account and definitely not all of it. I would've never been okay with that unless it was for an emergency, and even then, we would've figured out another way."

"Were you having money problems? Had a big expense come up that would've caused you to need that savings?"

"Two hundred thousand dollars?" I ask, my voice skeptical. "No, I think I would've remembered that."

"And it's not in your bank account?"

"I…" I pause. "I haven't actually checked our account since he disappeared." I guess that's one of the first things I should've done, now that I'm thinking about it. For all I know, he's cleaned us completely out of everything we own. For all I know, I'm officially broke. I'm not one of those wives who never looks at their accounts, but for the most part things come out automatically and neither of us has to check them that often. And neither of us check the investment account except once a year when we look to make sure we haven't lost it all. When we first invested, it became a habit to obsess over it constantly, but every time the market was down, we'd go into a panic, so we've learned to let it go and avoid checking it as much as possible.

And as for the main account, we look over it when we pay our bills or make a major purchase, but we've always been good about saving, so it's usually not something I think about, especially with so much on my mind. I put gas in the car with a credit card earlier without a second thought.

Tate wouldn't empty our account. Whatever is going on…he wouldn't leave us penniless, would he? He wouldn't leave us with nothing.

"Do you mind?" the detective asks, stepping closer.

"Yeah, sure." I nod, returning to the car to get my phone. Once I have it, I open up my banking app and log in. Relief floods my system when I see our accounts are untouched. "Everything looks the same, but the money from our investment account wasn't deposited into this one." I turn the phone back around so he can see it. "Maybe it takes a few days?"

He tucks his notebook back into his pocket. "Maybe. Not typically, but tell us if you see anything suspicious on your account. In the meantime, you might want to close those accounts and transfer the money into one with only your name on it. Just in case."

"Just in case…my husband tries to steal more from me?"

He doesn't respond except to continue staring at me, like that's answer enough.

"You don't think something bad has happened to him, then? You think he's stolen our money and left me? Skipped town? Ran away without saying good-bye?" The words wash over me as I say them, as real and painful as ever. It's getting harder and harder to deny that's what this looks like.

"They don't pay me to assume or to speculate. Until we find your husband, there's no way to know." He presses his lips together, turning to walk away, but stops and looks back at me. "We still don't have an explanation about the car accident, but, in looking at everything else— lying about a vacation and the missing money—well...in my experience, if it walks like a duck and talks like a duck, Mrs. Thompson, it's usually a duck." He does a sort of two-finger salute, then nods. "Take care of yourself. We'll be in touch." With another wave of his hand, he's back in the car and disappearing down the drive.

I gather my things, still shaken up over all that I've learned and head for the house. I don't know if I'm more furious or distraught as both emotions wage war inside of me, my stomach rumbling as if I might be sick. The back of my throat is thick with cotton, an unbearable feeling that I can't seem to be rid of. *How could he do this to me? Why would he do this to me?* Through it all, I want to believe there's a reason. That he was forced. That he did it to protect me somehow. But it doesn't make sense. He lied over and over, about the vacation, about the money.

I'm scared for him. Worried he's in danger and the police are spending so much time trying to figure out why he lied and accusing him of the things that by the time we find him, it'll be too late. I can't fathom the thought. I have to try harder, but I also can't be foolish or blinded by my love for him. I have to accept that he could've lied, that he *has* lied. That he could've left us.

I'm so torn about everything.

Tate wouldn't leave me.

Tate wouldn't lie.

Except that he did. And he has.

I'm reanalyzing every interaction we've had lately. Did he seem unhappy? Did he seem sad? When he told me goodbye that morning, did he seem like he was saying more than goodbye for the day? Did it feel like a final goodbye? How could he kiss me so casually, hold me for such a short time, if he knew it was going to be forever? Did I really mean so little to him? And what about the boys? How could he have not taken longer with them that morning? Said more? *How dare he do this to them!*

I'm still vacillating between rage and sadness as I make my way toward the front door, and Mom meets me.

"What was that about?" she asks, keeping her voice low.

I don't want to tell her. Somehow, I still want to protect Tate. If this is all, somehow, a misunderstanding, I want her to still love her son-in-law. At the same time, I hate myself for caring. For being so pathetic.

"He's the detective on Tate's case. Just giving me an update."

"And he had to come by to do that?"

I nod, walking past her. "I appreciate that he did. So we know they're still working on it and looking for him."

"So what was the update?" she asks, following behind me as I head for the kitchen.

I stop, keeping my voice low. "There's some money missing from our retirement account. They're trying to find out where it went."

"How much money?" Her eyes widen.

"Not much," I lie. "They'll track it down. Not a big deal." I wave her off, turning toward the kitchen again and not stopping until I have the boys in my arms. "How was school?" I bend down between them, where they're sitting at the kitchen table working on homework.

"Fine," Ryker says.

"Boring," Finley says. "Is Dad back yet?"

"Not yet," I tell them, trying to keep my voice light. "But hopefully soon, okay? Do you need help with your homework?"

"No," Ryker says. "We've got it. Mine's just social studies. And Finley's is science. Easy peasy."

"Easy peasy," I repeat, tears stinging my eyes. I look over at Finley, who has pictures of leaves cut out and scattered across the table, using a glue stick to place them with their matches on the sheet of paper in front of him. They're working so diligently, both unbothered by my presence and the lack of Tate's.

I stand up, patting my thighs as I do. "Okay, if you're sure. I'm going to change." Mom appears behind me, and I spin around. "I need to check in with my boss, too. Let me give her an update, and then I'll get supper going."

"Grandpa's bringing pizza home from work," Ryker says without looking up.

"You shouldn't be worried about your job at a time like this. Maybe now's the time to finally quit that place and come back to work for us. You know your dad would be thrilled to have you, and you can start once things have calmed down here." Her eyes light up with hope.

It kills me to tell them no every time they offer this, but at this moment, I'm grateful to have the option. I have no idea when I'll be able to go back to work, and if Margie fires me, I'm glad to have somewhere to go. "I know, Mom. Thanks, but we've talked about this. I've told you I'd love to work for you again, but The Bold Bean's hours fit the boys' school schedule better. I know Dad would give me the hours I need, but you guys need help on the weekends and evenings while I need to work during school hours."

"We could have you open at ten thirty, and work until three—"

"That's not enough hours, though. Besides, it wouldn't be fair of him to give me all the daytime shifts when other employees want them, too. You guys are even still there during the weekends and evenings. You deserve employees who can be there when you need them to."

She gestures toward the boys. "They could come with you. You always loved being there with us."

I squeeze her arm. "I appreciate the offer, always. And we can talk about it more later. Right now, they said Dad's bringing home pizza?"

She nods, but I can tell she's upset. "I hope that's okay. I was going to cook, but the boys couldn't agree on what they wanted, and pizza felt like an easy option. Your dad just went in to help with inventory, but he's going to bring pizzas home for everyone."

"Of course it's okay. It's more than okay, but you didn't have to do that."

She waves me off. "Oh, please. Your dad misses bringing you home pizza. When you were a little girl, when you'd go to the shop with him for the day right after we opened, he was like a kid in a candy store. And bringing it home for you, seeing how excited you got, it never got old for him." Her voice cracks, and she looks away, which just makes me tear up more.

My parents worked hard to open their pizza shop and keep it going. So much of my childhood was spent within that shop, learning more than I'd ever need to know about pizza or watching them work while I did my homework. Now it's successful enough that they have full-time help, but Dad is still there whenever he can be. "It makes him happy to have something to do." I suspect it makes her just as happy, but neither of us says as much. Having my parents take care of me, even as an adult, is still one of the most comforting things. I wonder if I'll ever grow out of that.

"Besides," she says, pulling me out of my thoughts, "Daphne and Lane will be over in an hour or so, and pizza's easy for everyone. You just go and do whatever you need to do. I've got the boys."

It's hard not to feel overwhelmed by my mom sometimes. She's vocal and pushy when she's made up her mind. Opinionated. She's always been a doer and a people pleaser, but I know she's trying her hardest to support me through an impossible situation, and right now all I want to do is cry and tell her 'thank you' a million times. If we make it through this, I will never complain about her to Tate again. Or even to myself.

I will never complain about her again.

"Thanks, Mom. Seriously."

She smiles at me with her lips tucked into her mouth, a sad smile that reminds me of all that is going wrong in my life, and I hug her quickly so she doesn't see the tears I feel stinging my eyes. "Of course. I just want to help, lovebug."

"I'll be back, okay?" Before she can answer, before my tears start to fall, I hurry down the hallway and into the bedroom, dusting them away as quickly as I can.

I can't fall apart right now. I have things to do.

Before I can give in to my tears, I set to work. The whole way home, I kept thinking of the photograph on Aaron's desk, the one with the lion tattoo on full display. I wonder if Tate has any photographs of the four of them together, anything that might help me gather insight into their friendship. I can't believe there is no connection between the men's friendship and what is going on today, and if I can find the connection, maybe I can find my husband.

In our closet, there's a box of old photographs I've been saying for years I'm going to buy albums for, yet I still haven't gotten around to it. On my tiptoes, I grab the box from the top of the closet and place it on the floor, dropping down to sort through them. I know there are a few from his college days, just like there are old prom photos from my high school years and pictures of me working at the pizza shop alongside Mom and Dad as my first job. Most of these pictures are from the years before Tate and I got married, before our phones became the only albums that exist.

I have so many fond memories of going through old photo albums with my mom and grandma when I was a kid, and I always promised myself I'd make sure the boys had that, that I wouldn't let their only memories become digital, but I've failed at that goal.

If Tate comes home, if he's okay, I promise to do better. I'll buy albums immediately. I'll print every photo on my phone. Every single one.

I sort through the photos quickly, placing mine in one pile and his in the other. Mine is much larger. There's only a small section of photos of him, with a few guys or girls in college. Tate's parents adopted him from foster care in high school, so there aren't any pictures of him as a child, which is another reason I've always wanted to make sure our children had plenty of pictures of their childhood.

Once all the pictures are sorted, I begin going through his photos slowly. There are less than fifty total, I'd guess. I stop on a photo of him with a group of boys. It's college; I recognize the insignia from Highland University on Tate's shirt. Their arms are draped around each other's shoulders, with a bonfire that's probably too large to be safe behind them.

I recognize the face of the man I saw in the photograph at the police station, and my eyes linger on him. There's so much life behind his eyes here, it makes me sad to think he's gone. He's the shortest of the group, with a thick neck and wild, dark hair. His cheeks are flushed red, but aside from having fewer wrinkles and no bruises or scrapes, he looks just as he did in those photos. There's no doubt this is Dakota Miller.

Next to him is the man I now know to be Aaron Bond. He has decidedly more hair and less pudge around his waist, but he's still completely recognizable. Tate is at the end, his gangly arm draped over the shoulder of Bradley Jennings. I recognize his face from the photos in the obituary I found.

But there is a fifth boy I don't recognize in the center of the photo, and it's him my eyes go to instantly. He's attractive, almost painfully so, even in the blurry photograph. Dark hair and eyes, and the only one in the photo not smiling.

I flip the photo over, hoping to find writing that might tell me who the boy is, but there's nothing. He was probably just one of the kids at the party that night, but I make a mental note to keep an eye out for his face in any other photos. If he comes up again, he could be in danger just as much as the others. Or—a worse thought crosses my mind—he could be the one causing the danger in the first place.

I could see it, now that the thought is there. There's a darkness lurking behind his eyes that makes me uncomfortable.

I scan the rest of the stack. There are a few photos of Tate at his dad's company during his summer internship, and a few of him in class or in his dorms. I search the photos, desperately looking for the face of that boy, but I don't find any others.

When I've gone through all the photos that belong to Tate, I tuck them back inside the photo box, keeping the one group photo out in hopes of asking my in-laws if they remember the boy in the middle, and make my way back into the kitchen. To my relief, my dad has just arrived with dinner. I didn't realize until right this moment that I can't remember the last time I ate, but it certainly wasn't today.

Grief has replaced my hunger, but I can't let that happen. I have to take care of myself, stay healthy for the boys' sake if nothing else.

The dinner table is full of chatter, with the boys each telling us about their day and asking about Tate, and my parents trying their hardest to keep the conversation in positive, safe territory. It feels like a betrayal of Tate to be sitting here having a meal together, as if we aren't missing him. As if every time I look toward his empty chair, my heart doesn't squeeze.

But it does.

Of course it does.

We aren't whole without him, and I'm not sure how I'll ever recover if he chose this. If he left us without answers on purpose.

When the door opens later, and Daphne and Lane arrive, they join us at the table, though their moods are decidedly more somber. When dinner is done, my parents put the boys to bed so we can catch up.

"What did you find out at the police station?" I ask, gathering the plates and carrying them across the room to the sink.

Daphne sighs. "Nothing, really. Just more of the same. They're working through several leads, but there's nothing concrete to tell us. We told them about the boys and gave them their names, but I'm not sure what they're doing with that information or if they'll try to contact Aaron. They didn't say."

"Did you ask about a search party?"

"We did. Right now, they don't seem to think it's a good idea," Lane says. "Apparently there isn't enough evidence of where he might be for there to be a good enough cause to use resources on a search party."

"Well, we could go look on our own," I suggest, though it feels strange. The police are right. He could be anywhere. "We don't need permission to do that. Maybe we could search around where the accident happened. Just in case he was in the car."

Daphne pinches her lips together, looking down. She sniffles, wiping her fingers under both eyes. "Oh, I think they're giving up on him, Celine."

"They're not," I promise her, reaching across and taking her hand. I want to tell them about the missing money, but I don't know how to without making it seem like I'm accusing Tate of something. "I promise they're not. We won't let them."

She nods, drying her eyes. "Thank you. Tate is so lucky to have you."

"I love him so much," I tell her.

"We know you do." She squeezes my hand.

"I actually have a question for you," I tell her, pulling the photo from my pocket. It's slightly crinkled now.

"What's this?" She takes the photo, staring down at it, then chokes back a sudden, unexpected sob and runs her finger across the paper. "Oh. Oh."

"I found it in Tate's things. These were the boys you said he was close with in college, right? Bradley, Dakota, and Aaron."

She nods with fat tears in her eyes. "I didn't know Tate still had this picture. They were all like sons to us. They were at our house all the time. Holidays, school breaks. Oh my gosh, they were all such pains, but...it was the closest thing we ever had to feeling like a complete family. I lived for times they were all there." She sniffles again, lost in thought as she stares down at the photo.

"What about this boy?" I point to the unnamed boy in the center of the picture. "Do you know who he is?"

She looks closer at the picture, lifting it toward the light and her face. "I don't think so." She hands the photo to Lane. "Do you recognize him?"

Lane hardly looks at the photo before shaking his head, hiding tears in his own eyes. He can't seem to look at the photo of his son.

"We aren't giving up on him," I promise them. "We're going to find Tate. He's going to be okay." I want that more than anything, for their sakes as much as mine. Even if he has stolen from me, even if he's leaving me, I just want to know he's okay.

A somber thought occurs to me then. If I lose him, if he's leaving me, will I lose his parents, too? Will they stop coming around as much? Will the boys lose them?

"Where did you find this anyway?" Daphne asks, tapping the photo in her hand.

"It was in a box of old photos we keep around. I figured out who the other boys were, but I couldn't place the fifth one."

"The three other boys were the friends we knew. The ones Tate was always hanging around with. But it doesn't surprise me that he included someone else in this photo. He was always so kind." She sniffles. "You know how he is. Makes friends everywhere he goes." She grabs a napkin from the holder in the center of the table and dabs her eyes, then her nose.

That does sound like Tate. He can make friends in line at the grocery store. I've literally seen it happen. As in, 'let's go out to dinner, come to our house for a cookout Saturday' kind of friends.

"Do you mind if I keep it?" she asks, holding her hand out. "I would—I mean, if you don't need it, I would really like to have it."

I hesitate, not wanting to give up even a tiny piece of my husband, but at the end of the day, I have no real attachment to the photograph, and it's clear my in-laws do. "Of course," I assure her. "It's yours."

Her chin quivers again as she looks down and dabs her eyes. "Thank you. I can't believe they're gone. My boys. My sweet boys."

She clutches the photo to her chest just as my father-in-law says, "We should get going, I think. Let the kids get some rest."

As soon as the words leave his mouth, he hesitates in his movements, as if he has glitched, and I know exactly what happened. Usually, when he says anything about 'the kids,' he's referring to Tate and me, and that weight sits in between us, heavy on his expression before he continues to stand up.

Losing one person is hard enough. Losing an entire photograph's worth of people, an entire group of people you love without having any answers—I don't even want to imagine.

Once we've said our goodbyes and they've left for the night, I find my dad in Ryker's room, reading to him, while my mom rocks Finley to sleep across the hall in the rocking chair we've had in his bedroom since before he was born.

I wave to them, letting them know I'll be right back, then head to my room to brush my teeth and change into my pajamas. It's weird here without Tate. I feel his absence in every part of the house and every moment of my life.

If he was here, he'd be stretched out on the bed, telling me about his day. Or staring at me in the mirror while he brushes his teeth, trying to make me laugh.

If he was here, it wouldn't hurt like this.

When I'm done, I grab the box of photos from the bed—still waiting for me to slip the photo I no longer have back inside of it—and move to put the lid back on, but something stops me.

It's a photograph I looked at earlier, one I assume was taken on the same night as the photo I gave Daphne. I'm only just noticing the jackets slung across chairs in the background, and the fact that three of them are letterman jackets.

My eyes scan the familiar names. Thompson. Jennings. And then the final name, one I don't recognize: Acri.

My heart stutters, and I grab my laptop, typing in his last name and the name of their school: Highland University.

The first few results don't give me much, but finally, I see an article that catches my attention. The coverage is small, just a paragraph, but it's enough to make my chest tight.

Local Boy Reported Missing From Campus

Late Saturday night, police responded to reports from students that they believed their classmate was missing from his dorm. It is now confirmed police are looking for senior Matteo Acri. No word yet on what police believe to have happened or if they believe Acri may be in danger. This is a developing story. Anyone with any information is encouraged to call the Dublin County Police Department.

I read the article two more times, trying to make sense of it, then search Matteo Acri's name on its own, hoping to discover a report that he was found alive and well, but the search turns up nothing. No updates were ever posted, which likely means he was never found.

I close my laptop with a heavy sigh.

Five friends. Two are dead. Two are missing. It can't be a coincidence any longer...can it?

CHAPTER FIFTEEN

TATE

Day of Disappearance

I'm itching to check my phone, though it's still at the office. This time I tucked it into my desk drawer, so Dustin won't find it.

"We have to move the body," Dakota says, drawing me out of my thoughts as he picks at the fries on his plate.

It's the most ridiculous plan I've ever heard. "Are you kidding me?"

"If someone knows what we did, if Aaron snitches, if the cops come around asking questions, we have to be able to deny it. If he can point the police right to the body, how on earth are we going to do that?"

"It's been more than twelve years. How much of a body would even be left?"

"Enough to send you to prison." His voice is firm and matter-of-fact. It sends chills down my spine.

"How would we even get on to campus without anyone noticing? And then dig up a grave? It's impossible. No. No way. It's too risky."

He dips a fry in ketchup and pops it into his mouth. "Leaving it where we left it, where other people know where it is, is too risky. Anything else is playing it safe."

I scowl at him, my gaze searing into his. "If I didn't know any better, I'd say you wanted me to get caught. That you're trying to set me up."

He laughs, rolling his eyes. "Dude, I'm literally offering to help you. I don't know what else you want from me."

"Why are you trying to help me?" I ask. "We both know it's not out of the kindness of your heart."

He has the decency not to look offended as he says, "I've moved on from everything that happened back then. I've tried to forget it and build a good life. From what I can tell, you have too. I've been the one trying to get us back together. We were friends, and maybe the rest of you don't care, but I do. That night doesn't ruin all the rest of it, does it?"

"Of course it does." I drop my hands flat on the table. "Of *course* it does. I can't just pretend it didn't happen."

"Fine." He's angry now, but so am I. We're just too different. We always have been. "But either way, we're in this together. And the only way we can be sure we

137

can leave this behind is if we move the body and hide any last evidence. If whoever is behind all of this doesn't know where the body is, they have no proof of anything. Just their word against ours." I know he means Aaron, know he still thinks this is all his doing, but I don't. I still can't believe Aaron would do anything like this. I can't believe he'd kill Bradley, that he'd follow and try to scare Dakota. He may be afraid, but he isn't a monster. Once, we were his brothers. Even after all this time, that means something.

But either way, and regardless of how I feel, Dakota is right. The only way to know for sure we're safe, is to get rid of any evidence that could be used against us.

"Okay, I have a plan."

He leans forward. "Hit me with it."

"We're going to swap vehicles," I tell him.

Apprehensively, he shakes his head. "What are you talking about? Why?"

"Because you're being followed," I remind him. "If we take your truck there, someone could follow us and see what we're doing."

A muscle in his jaw twitches. "So we'll take your car and leave my truck in a parking lot somewhere."

"No. It's too risky. What if someone sees us both get into my car?"

He leans forward against the table, pinning me with a hard stare. "What if someone sees us swapping cars? It's the same amount of risk."

I gesture toward his head. "Give me your hat, then.

You're shorter and your hair's a different cut, but we'll cover the hair up with a hat and move quickly. From a distance, I can probably pass as you."

"Only if you've gained forty pounds since we came in here." He's staring at me strangely, not sold on the idea, but he isn't completely shutting it down anymore. I can sell this if I work hard enough.

"It'll be okay. This is the best way to get this done. I'll take your truck and drive around, distract whoever is following you. You take my car and go to campus. I'll keep whoever it is distracted, and you can move the body."

"Why can't we just keep our own cars, and *you* move the body?"

Because I don't totally trust you.

Because I don't want to be involved.

"Because you're stronger than I am, first of all. You'll be able to get it done faster, and also because I want to see the person who's following you. If you want me to believe that's happening, I need to see it. And if you want me to trust that you're truly trying to help me and not set me up, you need to be the one who moves it. It was your idea."

His gaze narrows at me. "How do I know you won't be setting *me* up?"

Thinking quickly, I say, "How do you want me to prove it?"

He's always been easily manipulated. I just have to

hope he makes this easy on us both. There's no way I'm going anywhere near that body ever again.

He thinks for a moment, chewing on the inside of his lip as his eyes search the room. Finally, he lights up. "I want your phone. And your wallet."

"What for?"

"So I have proof you're coming back for me. If the police catch me out there, I have proof we were working together. I'll say you were just here and ran off." He tilts his head to the side, challenging me. "If you're not setting me up, it shouldn't be a problem."

"You don't need my wallet and phone. This was your plan, and this is the only way to get it done. And we can't trust Aaron, or I'd ask him to drive your truck so I could come help you. If you think moving the body is the best way, this is our only chance. Besides, my phone is back at the office."

"So, we'll go and get it. I'm not doing this without some sort of show of faith. Your wallet and phone, or no deal."

I sigh. I have no idea how I'm going to explain a trip to my old college in our location app to Celine, but that's a problem for later.

"Fine. Whatever. Deal."

A beat passes, and finally, a smile cracks across his lips and he holds out his hand. "Don't fuck me on this, brother."

I dip my head down, taking his hand and shaking it

over the table. "Come on. You know me better than that."

CHAPTER SIXTEEN

CELINE

For a long time, I resist the urge to look anything else up. Whatever happened all those years ago, I have no proof that it has anything to do with what's happening now.

Maybe I'm just in denial. Maybe I don't want to believe it. I have all of the pieces to a confusing puzzle, but without actual answers about what happened back then, Matteo Acri's disappearance in college does not explain why Tate stole our money and disappeared now.

There is nothing concrete that proves it's connected other than Aaron being shady, and even that could just be coincidence or the cowardly act of someone who hasn't spoken to my husband in years and doesn't want to get involved in a criminal investigation.

I don't want to make a mistake by getting sidetracked, but I also don't want to give up on a lead that feels promising.

After my parents leave, I lie in bed and remind myself of this over and over and over again. I toss and turn, unable to get the story out of my head. Why wouldn't Tate have told me his friend went missing in college? Wasn't that the sort of thing that came up once in a while?

Maybe Daphne was right, though. Maybe they weren't actually all that close. Maybe he just happened to be there when they were taking a picture, and the boys didn't want to be rude so they included him. I wish I had the ability to ask the rest of them, that there was anyone still around who might be more helpful than Aaron.

I should probably bring this information to the police, but really, what information do I have? A bunch of disconnected pieces to a puzzle that doesn't match. Even with several of them missing or dead, none of it means anything unless I find a connection deeper than a friendship from a decade ago. Everything I've brought to the police so far has been dismissed. I don't want to distract them with things that aren't certain when they need to be focusing on Tate.

When I can't bear another second of the silence and the raging questions in my head, I roll over and grab my laptop from the nightstand, searching the internet for Matteo's name again.

I have to scroll to the fifth page of results before I

find something new, and it's a single mention of him in another article.

I click on it and read through, shock flooding my system.

In the days after Matteo's disappearance, the police were called to campus after a few students found a body they believed could be Matteo's. It was charred beyond recognition—that's the actual word the article used, *charred*. But it later turned out to be a professor. A female professor named Aubrey Vance. Between Matteo's disappearance and Professor Vance's murder, two crimes happening so close together on the same campus, the atmosphere on campus had begun to get unsettling, and students and families alike were feeling unsafe. The article doesn't say anything else about whether they discovered what happened or caught the culprit.

When I search her name, I find several memorial articles about her, mentioning what a wonderful professor she was. Though it was just her first year teaching, it looks like the school dedicated a library to her after her death, but as far as I can tell, her killer was never caught.

On a whim, I look up the writer of one of the articles, and when I find an email address for someone I believe to be him on LinkedIn, I send him an email, letting him know I have some questions about her and would love the chance to chat with him.

I spend the next hour looking for anything that

might help me figure out if Tate had anything to with any of this, but there's nothing. He had to have known, though, right? They were in school together. He would've known them both most likely. If he didn't have a class with the professor, he would've at least heard about her death.

I can't believe he never told me about any of this.

The more I learn about my husband's past, the more I realize how little I ever really knew him.

CHAPTER SEVENTEEN

TATUM

Highland University
Twelve Years Ago

"Party's here!" I shout, cupping my hands around my mouth. I step out of the car and pop the trunk. The thing is loaded to the brim with boxes of beer, Mad Dog 20/20, Boone's Farm, and 99 Bananas.

Stupid fruity shit for the girls and beer for us.

The house is packed already—loud music blaring, lights inside flashing every color. A group of guys rush over on command and unload the car, bringing it all inside after me. Dakota has some girl on his lap on the couch, and Aaron is close by, playing video games with a group of nerds. It takes me a minute to find Bradley, but eventually I see he's already passed out on a chair in the corner. I grab a girl's arm as I pass. "Sharpie," I bark.

It takes her too long to realize what I've said, but eventually, she nods. "Oh, sure. Just a sec." When she comes back, she hands me the Sharpie, and I cross the room, drawing a cock on Bradley's cheek, the tip near his lips. *Stupid fucker.*

I toss the Sharpie at the girl, not checking to see if she catches it.

"Hey, Tatum. Wanna play?" Aaron calls, holding out his controller.

I ignore him, making my way into the kitchen. *God, I wish my friends weren't such losers. I've got to get out of this shithole town.*

"Tate, my man! What's up! You killed it at the game the other night!" some idiot calls as I walk through the kitchen.

I spin on my heels, glaring at him. "What did you call me?"

The kid stops, his eyes shifting to the friends surrounding him. "Um, Tate?"

I grab the front of his shirt, balling it into a fist just under his chin. I would slam his head into the wall if I was in a bad mood, but he's not worth it. "Do I know you?"

"Hey! Hey! I didn't mean anything by it, bro." His hands are up in surrender.

"Do *not* shorten my name. Nicknames are for lazy punks and little girls, dickwipe. My fucking name is Tatum."

"I'm sorry," he says again.

147

I shove him backward, releasing his shirt at once. "Don't ever fucking speak to me. Do you hear me? Don't even look at me."

He nods, eyes on the ground at my words, and like lightning, the group scatters. When I turn around, the rest of the room parts for me. People are so easy, man. Just one little conversation, and suddenly, we're all on the same page.

I walk through the room without a look toward any of them, but they're all looking at me. They don't exist, and I'm the entire world.

My dick aches, and I need to get off, so eventually I start scanning the crowd, trying to decide who the lucky lady will be tonight. I've had most of these girls already and want fresh blood.

Jogging up the stairs, I listen at the first door, and when I hear the sounds of moaning, I push inside, flipping on the light.

"Hey!" a girl cries, covering herself. The dude underneath her grabs the blanket.

"What the fuck, man?"

"Out!" I shout, jutting a thumb over my shoulder.

It takes a second for them to realize who I am—and more importantly that they don't want to fuck with me —and when they do, they both jump up off the bed. The guy is out of the room first, and I grab the girl's arm. "Not you. Get back on the bed."

"What?" Her eyes widen.

Actually, now that I've gotten a good look at her,

she's not that hot anyway. Her nose is too big, and her breath smells like ass. I push her forward. "Forget it. Get out of here."

She scampers out of the room, throwing her shirt over her head. Not like anyone cared to see those tiny tits anyway. She could've walked through the house naked, and no one would've batted an eye.

I check the second room, which has some dude choking on his own vomit in bed. *Not my problem.* Shutting the door, I make my way into the next room, where I stop in my tracks.

The two figures on the bed wrench away from each other in the lamplight, covering themselves with their hands.

"Well, well, well…what do we have here?" I click my tongue, surveying the scene.

"Get the fuck out of here, Tatum." Matteo jumps up from bed, throwing a blanket across the woman's bare body and stalking toward me, completely naked, his finger outstretched toward the door.

I look down at the wimpy, half-hard dick pointed in my direction, then back up with a chuckle. "At ease, soldier. Is little Mafia Matteo getting down and dirty with the teacher? Why didn't you tell us how you were getting extra credit? I want in."

"Back off, asshole," he shouts, pointing toward the door. "Didn't your parents teach you to mind your own business? Oh, wait. Forgot you don't have those."

"You're one to talk." I smirk. "Seriously, I want in on

149

this." I start unbuttoning my pants, stalking toward the bed. Professor Vance is hot, but I never thought she'd be into students.

"Not a chance," she says with a sneer, pulling the blanket up higher on her chest.

"We're not just hooking up, asshole," Matteo says. "It's not a game. We're dating."

My eyes widen, and I cross my arms. "Well, pardon the fuck out of me. Why haven't you mentioned this? Does the dean know?"

Matteo moves to stand in front of her, pulling shorts on finally. "She's not my professor. I'm not taking any of her classes on purpose. We went to school together. She was a few years older, a senior when I was a freshman, and we were friends then. We started talking when I found out she was coming to teach here this year. Thought I'd give her the lay of the land."

I eye her. "You're certainly giving her the lay of something."

"Enough. No jokes. None of your shit tonight. I'm not in the mood. I've said she's off-limits, okay? Why don't you run along and torture some underclassman?"

"Oh, but this is much more fun."

His jaw tics. "Fun's over."

"Come on, Professor V, what do you say?" I wink. "I've seen what he's working with now. I promise I'm a lot more exciting."

"Out, asshole!" Matteo bellows, shoving me back-ward and getting truly angry for the first time.

I laugh. Pissing my dickhead friends off is probably my favorite thing to do, especially Moody Mafia Matteo. Maybe I'll add that "Moody" to his official title. He hates when I call him Mafia Matteo, which I've been doing for years, ever since I found out he's Italian, but tough luck. It's funny, and you've gotta admit when jokes are good, even when they're at your expense. Or, maybe you don't, but it won't stop me from saying it. "Maybe you should lock your doors from now on," I say, buttoning my pants back up.

"Maybe you should knock on doors that aren't your own."

"Calm your tits. I'm going." I cast a look back at Professor Vance. "As for you, I'll see you Monday during office hours, hmm? I'm thinking I'll need a lot of assistance."

Neither of them say a word to me as I walk out of the room, which pisses me the fuck off. I wasn't even that pissed at first, more amused than anything, but no one talks to me that way, and no one turns me down. I slam the door shut and punch a hole straight through it, smiling when I hear her scream. Blood pours down my hand from my knuckles, and I grab the first girl I see, pushing her into an empty bedroom and onto the bed. She doesn't argue as I unbutton my pants—they never do—but it's not what I want.

She's not what I want.

And, if there's one thing everyone knows about Tatum Thompson, it's that I always get what I want.

CHAPTER EIGHTEEN

CELINE

As soon as the hour is reasonable, I dial my mother-in-law's number, and when she answers, I say the name that has been replaying in my mind over and over all night.

"Matteo Acri," I blurt out.

"Celine?" she asks, sounding half asleep. "What did you say? Was that a sneeze? Or a...spell? Are the boys watching *Harry Potter* again?"

"No, I said Matteo Acri. I think that was the name of the other boy in the picture I gave you."

She pauses. "The photo from last night?"

"Yes. Does that name sound familiar?"

"I don't think so." Her voice goes muffled. "Honey, do we know a..." She pauses, her voice coming back to me. "What did you say it was again, Celine?"

"Matteo Acri," I repeat.

"Matteo Acri," she tells Lane. "Celine thinks he's the other boy in the picture."

"Acri…" I can hear him mumbling in the distance through the line. "I don't think so."

"We don't think so, honey, but maybe. What did you find out about him?"

"Nothing, really. Just an article. But there was something. He, um, he went missing when they were in school."

Daphne gasps. "Oh my gosh, yes! I do remember that. The boy who went missing. Yes. Oh, yes." She's quiet for a second. "I don't remember if they ever found him. That was so awful."

"I couldn't find anything about it if they did."

"That's just terrible." Suddenly, she's crying.

"Do you think he and Tate were close?"

"Oh." She sniffles. "I don't think so, no. I don't remember Tate mentioning him other than when he went missing. And honestly, we might've just heard about that on the news or something. I can't even say for sure he's the one who told us."

"Oh, okay. He must've just been around the night they took that picture, then."

"I think so, too. If you find out anything else, though, let us know. I'll try to keep thinking about it in case there's anything else I might remember."

"Okay, thanks. And I will. I'll keep you posted." We end the call, and I slip out of bed, determination running through my veins. In the hall, my parents are there again and have just begun to wake the boys up.

"Good morning, sweetheart," Mom says. "You could've slept in."

"I have some errands to take care of this morning," I tell her. I'm planning to run to the bank to close our accounts and open new ones, but I don't want to tell Mom and Dad about that. Not yet, anyway. Foolish as it may be, some part of me is still holding out hope for this to all be a simple misunderstanding.

As if Tate might just walk back in the door with bags of groceries and say he forgot how to get home or got locked in a coat closet at work or something. The realistic side of me knows that isn't what's going to happen, but the part of me who is still very much in love with her husband, the part that so desperately wants her children's father here with us, isn't ready to give up the hope just yet.

Once the boys are up and dressed, I give them hugs and kisses, promising to give them an update on Daddy as soon as we have it and then thank my parents for taking them to school again.

Yesterday I hated that they were going, but today I'm very thankful for the consistency in our routine as I get ready and make my way out the door.

As I cross the driveway and approach the car, I spot an email appear on my phone and open it quickly when I see the name.

Conroy Langdon, the man I emailed last night.

My heart leaps as I skim over his email.

Celine,

I'd be more than happy to answer any questions you have about Aubrey Vance. She was a dear friend, and I'm still sad we don't have answers or justice for her. I'd love to meet for coffee to discuss if you're around the Dublin area. What do you say?

Thanks,
Conroy

I respond quickly, giving him a few different coffee places in between us and head to the bank.

Once there, I'm nearly certain they think I'm the one trying to steal from my husband, but they do what I'm asking of them anyway, closing the old accounts and opening new ones with only my name on them. It shouldn't be this easy, but it really is. If Tate had wanted to, he could've taken everything. And if he does come back, if this is all just a misunderstanding or if he has a good explanation for it, I'm going to have to explain myself for this and hope he understands.

"And you're sure there were no deposits coming into the old accounts?" I confirm for the third time, hoping they'll see the investment money pending.

"No ma'am," the banker, Lauren, says, "nothing yet. But as I told you, if anything does try to come in over the next thirty days, it will reopen the account. After that, it will be kicked back, and you'll have to contact the payer directly to have it rerouted, so you definitely want to get everything switched over to the new account before those thirty days are up."

"Okay, great." I nod, gathering the paperwork back up. "I will."

"And if you decide to add anyone else to the account, you can just bring them in."

"Right, thanks."

"We recommend adding a POD beneficiary at a minimum, so that if something happens to you, there's a path for where the money should go. Otherwise, it's a fight in the courts, even with a will in place."

"Thanks," I say. "I'll keep that in mind." If she even knew what my life was like right now, she might realize that sounded a bit like a threat. *If something happens to you...*

When I leave the bank, I finally call my insurance agent back to get an update on Tate's car, which seems like it's on its way to being totaled—probably the best possible outcome in this situation—and the check should be in the mail within the next week.

I'm feeling as accomplished as I can be when a new email from Conroy comes in. He's agreed to meet me at a coffee shop an hour away from here, so I fire off a reply to let him know I'm on my way and hop in the car.

It feels a little bit like cheating on The Bold Bean

when I arrive at Jitters Coffee House, but I find the space cozy and inviting, despite my nerves. Conroy Langdon is waiting for me at a table near the back. He looks just like his photo, unlike the people who use headshots from ten years ago. He's wearing a suit and sporting thick, blond hair and a kind smile. When I approach the table, he holds out a hand for me.

"I'm sorry. I didn't know your coffee order, or I would've gotten you something."

"That's okay." I wave him off, sitting down at the two-seater table. "Thank you for meeting with me."

"Of course. To be honest, I was shocked when I got your email. I haven't heard the name Aubrey Vance in over a decade. You said you found my article about her death online?"

I nod. "Yes, and I looked you up and found your LinkedIn. I hope that's okay."

"More than okay. Can I ask why you were looking into her? Are the two of you related?"

I shake my head. "No, I didn't know her. I just..." I pause, trying to decide how to address this. "Because there is literally no better way to say this, I'll just be honest. Something strange is going on, and I was going down a rabbit hole that led me to discover Aubrey's obituary."

"A rabbit hole." He blows on his cup of coffee, lifting it to his lips and taking a sip. "Color me intrigued. Tell me more."

"My husband is missing." Those words never get easier to say.

His eyes flick to the wedding ring on my finger. "I'm so sorry to hear that."

"Thank you. And when I was looking into some of his friends, I found out about Aubrey, and well, now here I am. I know it's going to sound crazy, but part of me is starting to think this all could be related somehow."

The wrinkle in his forehead deepens. "Related? How do you mean?"

"My husband went to school at Highland, and by coincidence or not, most of his friends are now either dead or missing. Aubrey was found just after the first of his friend group went missing."

His brows crinkle together. "Missing? Wait a second, you don't...do you mean Matteo Acri?"

"You knew him?"

"It's a small school," he says. "Matteo's disappearance was a big deal. The talk of the campus for quite a while." He pauses. "Forgive me, who is your husband?"

"Tate, um, Tatum Thompson."

The man's face pales, and he nearly drops his coffee cup, sloshing the light brown liquid down over the side. He hardly seems to notice the spill. "I guess I should've realized from your last name, but it's a common one, so I didn't think about it. You're telling me you actually *married* Tatum Thompson?"

"I guess you knew him too, then."

He looks away, appearing to try and collect himself. "He made sure of it." If I didn't know better, I'd say there's a hint of bitterness in his voice.

"What do you mean? You and Tate didn't get along?"

He opens his mouth, then closes it, thinking. "I'm sorry that he's missing. Truly, I am, but Tatum Thompson as I knew him was an awful, awful bully to everyone around him."

That doesn't sound like Tate at all. I bite my lip. "We all make mistakes in college." Not that I would know, I guess. I never went.

He nods, taking another sip of his coffee. Upon finally noticing the spill, he grabs a napkin and dabs it off the side of his cup and the tabletop. "What I can tell you is that Professor Vance was always very kind. Very well respected at our school. Her loss was a terrible one."

"And what about Matteo?"

He balls the napkin up and sets it aside. "I didn't know him as well, but he was never impolite to me. A bit shy, maybe. He kept to his circle. I was sorry to hear he disappeared but—" He cuts himself off.

"But what?"

"Well, forgive me again, but to be frank, I always suspected your husband and his friends of having something to do with it."

My blood chills. "What do you mean?"

He takes a sip of his coffee, letting the heavy silence linger. "It was just a theory, but quite a few people in school thought it. Tatum left school right after, but that school was his kingdom. Several of us believed he never would've left unless he was guilty and had something to hide."

I bristle at his comments. I knew Tate left school during his last semester, but his parents told me it was because he went to study abroad. Was that a lie? It's no wonder Tate never spoke about who he was back then. He's changed so much for the better, but now I wonder if it's because of a terrible mistake he made back then. "I'm sorry he was so awful to you, truly. He's different now. He's a kind husband, a good father."

The man looks at me as if he pities me. "I hope that's true. I really do. And I'd never wish ill on him. But if you ask me, only a handful of people know what happened to Matteo Acri back then. If you ask me, he's dead, and your husband and his friends at the very least know what happened, and, at the worst, were responsible."

The weight of what he's saying washes over me because he doesn't know everything yet.

"Tate's friends? Do you mean Bradley Jennings and Dakota Miller?"

"And Aaron something. I can't remember his last name."

"Bond."

He nods. "Yep, that was it. Why?"

"Because everyone except Aaron is dead or missing now," I say with a swallow. "Including Tate."

CHAPTER NINETEEN

TATUM

Twelve Years Ago

"Hey there, sweetheart," Mom greets us at the door, arms spread wide for a hug. I lean down quickly, giving her a pat on the back.

"'Sup?"

"I'm so happy you boys could stay with us for the holiday," she says, walking over to the guys and hugging Matteo first, stretching up on her toes to reach her arms around his neck.

Matteo squeezes her and lifts her off the ground until she squeals with delight. "Thanks for inviting us, Mrs. T."

He places her on the ground, and she tugs at the bottom of her shirt, shaking her head ruefully. "Oh, please. You know you're all welcome here anytime."

She moves to hug Aaron next, then Bradley, and finally Dakota.

"It's so good to have a house full. Holidays were always much too quiet before this one came along." She bumps her hip in my direction, and the guys all laugh. "I have the guest rooms all made up, so you'll be comfortable, but just let me know if you need anything at all."

Matteo sets his bag down. "Oh, here." He reaches inside the duffel to grab a bottle of wine and a book. He hands them to my mom, and with the way she takes it, you'd think it was a fucking bar of gold.

"Oh, sweetheart, you didn't have to—"

"Merry Christmas. It's from all of us. I mean, it's not much, but we wanted to get you something to say thanks for letting us stay."

She's all teary-eyed as she hugs them again, and I roll my eyes, stalking to my room without another word. *I don't need to be down there for that little love fest. Jesus Christ. Get a fucking room, why don't you?* I drop my bag on my bed and kick my shoes off.

Mom's using some new fabric softener that's too strong and makes my eyes water, so I take the comforter off the bed and toss it in a pile on the floor.

A few more minutes pass before I hear the assholes climbing the stairs and then slipping into their bedrooms. Bradley and Aaron will room together, and Dakota and Matteo, like usual. I'm half tempted to make them all leave after that little performance they put on downstairs. What the fuck was that about? Since when do they give Mom presents *before* Christmas even starts? It's bad enough they give her anything at all, the little kiss-asses.

I jerk my door open, slamming it into the wall, then stomp across the hall and shove Dakota's door open. They're both standing next to the beds my parents bought for them to sleep in when they stay over— which is all the fucking time, thanks to me, and they'd better not forget it.

"Easy, bro. Knock much?" Dakota asks, already unpacking his bag like he owns the place.

"I don't have to knock in my own fucking house, asshole," I shout. "You'd know that if any of you had houses of your own."

"Hey," Matteo warns, keeping his voice low, clearly shocked.

"I was kidding." Dakota's expression has gone serious, and both of them are looking at me now. "What's your problem?"

"My problem? Oh, I don't know." I wave my hand in the direction of the door. "What the shit was that?"

He stops unpacking, turning to face me. "What was what?"

"That shit you all pulled downstairs. Why the fuck are you buying my mom gifts and giving them to her when you get here like little 1950s housewives?"

Their brows draw down, and Dakota looks toward

the door. "Why is it a problem? We were just trying to be nice."

"They're my parents, not yours. You don't buy them gifts except for on holidays, and in case you're too stupid to read a calendar, Christmas is *not* today."

His hands go up. "I'm not trying to take your parents, Tatum. Fucking chill, man. We were just trying to be polite. It was a cheap bottle of wine and a book Matteo said she'd like. It's not a big deal, dude."

"It is a big deal if I say it's a big deal, so don't. Don't be polite. Just be who you are, or you won't be getting invited back. I don't care what she says. I'm the one who invites you. I'm the one who says you can stay. The second I change my mind, you're out."

"Were you really bothered by the fact that she said we could come here anytime?" Matteo asks, stepping forward. "Why do you care? It's not a competition, bro."

"You're damn right it's not, and you know why?" I jerk forward, my face in his. "Because I already won. And you'd better not forget it."

"What's going on?" Bradley's whiny little voice cuts through the room, and I spin around to face him.

"None of you asked permission to get my mom an extra gift, that's what's going on."

Bradley's eyes travel to Dakota, then to Matteo. "I didn't know we needed to ask permission. It's...I mean, it's Christmas." I want to smack the stupid little grin off his face.

"It's Christmas in *my* house. With *my* parents. Are you trying to make me look bad? You want them to think you're better than me and adopt you instead?"

It's Matteo who steps up. "Dude, first of all, we're all twenty-two. No one is trying to get adopted anymore. Not to mention that we're your friends. Your brothers. We aren't trying to *steal* your parents." He says it as if it's a stupid idea, which just pisses me off more. "No one was happier for you when you were adopted than we were. We all wanted better for you. Just because you were adopted and we weren't, doesn't mean we're trying to steal your family, so just take a breath and chill, okay? You're being ridiculous."

"Am I? Am I really? I got out, and you didn't. I got a family, and you didn't. Growing up, we all wanted this, and I got it. Don't think I don't know you all hate me for that," I tell him, my lips tight and unmoving. They think I'm an idiot, that I don't know they'd kill to be me. To have all that I have.

"Is that really what you think?" Aaron asks, his brows pinched together in that way that always makes him look constipated.

"It's what I know. You all want to be like me. You have since we were kids, bouncing from one foster family to the next. You followed me to the university I chose. You're always here with the family who chose me. You may as well tape yourselves to my ass at this point."

"We followed you, we hang out with you, because

167

we're friends," Dakota says, his expression pinched and exasperated, arms out to the sides. "We were the closest thing to brothers any of us had. Friends, Tatum. Remember that? Though right now I can't remember why."

There's a grumble of agreement, and I cock my head to the side. "Is that really how you feel?"

"No. Guys, stop. We should all just calm down," Bradley says. "It's Christmas. We shouldn't fight. We're just tired."

"No. You know what? Matter of fact, get out." I snap my fingers and point toward the door. "I want you out. Now."

"What?" Dakota asks. "You aren't serious."

"I couldn't be any more serious if I was Sirius fucking Black, dude. Get out of my house. I don't want you here anymore."

"You can't do that. You don't mean it. Come on, we always spend Christmas together," Aaron says. Clearly, he thinks I'm going to change my mind. That I should care what they think or want. What the fuck do they think this is, a circle jerk? Fucking therapy? *They'd like that, wouldn't they? Pussies.*

I give a single tight shake of my head. "Not anymore. Get out."

"He doesn't want us here. Let's just leave." Matteo is already stuffing things back into his bag, but the three others remain still.

"Come on, man. You're just mad. You don't mean

this," Bradley says, walking toward me. He puts his hand on my shoulder, and I snap. My fist whirls back, and I throw it forward, connecting with his face. Blood splatters everywhere and cascades down his face, and I can feel specks of it coating mine.

I blink. Then, everyone jumps into action all at once.

"Dude, what the fuck?" Dakota shouts, rushing forward, and soon there are hands and arms everywhere, trying to separate me from everyone else.

"*What is going on?*" Mom shouts, her voice cutting through the room. Everyone falls still, the entire room turning to face her as if we're in a military lineup and she's our drill sergeant. She takes a deep breath, staring at the mess we are.

"Mind your business," I growl.

Mom's cheeks flush bright pink, and I can tell I've humiliated her in front of everyone. Slowly, with Matteo leading the way, the boys all move to stand beside her, and Dakota leans down. "We're going to go, Mrs. T. We're sorry to have caused problems at Christmas."

Fat tears fill her eyes. "What? No. Don't go. Please, don't go. It won't feel like Christmas without all of my boys here."

My so-called brothers look at me, waiting for me to stop her tears, to end this fight. They want me to give in, but apparently they don't know me at all. They want me to give in? Fine. But not in the way they want. I'm going to make them all come crawling back to me.

"Fine, you want your boys?" I wrinkle my nose in disgust. "Have 'em. But you just lost this one." And with that, I'm gone.

I'm her only boy. I'm the one she chose. And I'm going to make sure she regrets forgetting that.

CHAPTER TWENTY

CELINE

When I get home, everything I've learned over the past few days is ready to come bubbling out of me.

Since Tate's disappearance, I've really tried to make it look like I have it together, but it couldn't be further from the truth. Maybe I've been lying to everyone, including myself, but right now, all I want to do is sleep. And cry. I want my mom to hold me and promise that somehow this is all going to be okay. That the man I knew wasn't a con artist who had me fooled, that his family would've told me who he really was, that they love me like a daughter and would protect me if they thought he was capable of hurting me, of hurting our sons.

I need someone else to say these things to me because I'm not sure I'm capable of saying them to myself anymore. I've tried so hard, but my resolve is slipping. I need help. I need someone to be here for me, and it can't just be me anymore.

I feel weak for even admitting that. I made it all of two days, and already I'm cracking under the pressure and weight of the pain. People have it so much worse than this.

They really do.

I shouldn't be so weak.

I'm on the verge of tears when I walk into my house. The boys come running up to me before I see my parents lingering in the doorway to the kitchen, and I promise myself I can hold it together for just a few more hours. For them.

I sink to the floor and hug my sons, hoping I can love them enough for the two of us. Hoping someday I will be enough for them, that what their father has done to us won't hurt so badly.

"Is Dad home yet?" Finley asks, releasing me to look around my shoulder like Tate might just pop out from behind the door.

"Not yet," I say, rubbing a hand down his arm. "How was your day?"

"Fine. Otis has a new Sonic toy, and I want one too."

I smile, wishing desperately it could always be this simple. That a toy could solve all of life's problems. I squeeze his hand. "Sure. We'll look for it, okay?"

He nods and bounds off to my dad. "She said yes!" He bounces up on his tiptoes, and my dad laughs, running a hand over his hair.

My in-laws walk out of the kitchen together then, and I hate myself because my immediate reaction is to be disappointed that they're here, but why shouldn't they be here? We're their family too, and right now, we're all they have. So I bite down the urge to pull my mom into my bedroom and spend the night crying, and instead put on the best brave face I can, and ask if they've already eaten.

To my relief—and to compound my guilt—Daphne and Lane picked up dinner from a restaurant on their way. While my dad helps the boys with their baths and to get ready for bed, I sit with Mom, Daph, and Lane, and eat in strained silence. They all just keep staring at me as if they're waiting for me to fall apart, as if they can sense that I'm no longer holding it together as well as I've been pretending.

When I go to take our dishes away after our meal, Mom stops me.

"How are you?" she asks, studying my face.

I want to tell her the truth, but I can't right now. "As well as can be expected, I guess."

"How did things go on your errands?"

"Fine." I narrow my eyes at her, realizing she's not waiting for me to crack after all. From the expectant looks on all of the faces in the room, I'd say they have something to tell me. "What is it? Just tell me."

"Nothing, sweetheart. We just wanted to be here for you," Daphne says. "With...today and everything. However we can. We want to support you."

"Today?" The way she's put emphasis on the word makes me think today is something special, but I have no idea what...

August 2nd.

Today is Tate's and my eleventh wedding anniversary, and I had no idea.

"Our anniversary." I sink down in the chair behind me. "I hadn't even realized it was today. I signed all the papers at the bank, wrote out the date, and I never even realized..."

"The bank?" Lane asks, obviously concerned.

"Just errands," I say, not wanting to get into it, and especially not with him. "I can't believe I forgot."

"You've had a lot on your mind," Mom says, rubbing my shoulder. "We're sorry we brought it up. We thought you must know and that today would be really hard on you. We didn't mean to make it worse."

"Tate would want us to be with you while he can't be," Daphne says. "I know wherever he is, he wishes he was here." She touches my shoulder next, and we're a triangle of pain and sadness in varying degrees. "What can we do for you?" she asks.

"Nothing." I shake my head. "Really, nothing. It's too hard to think about. I just...I think I want to be alone tonight." Guilt tears through me as I worry I've come across as rude after all they've done for me. I stand up. "Truly, thank you, guys, for being here. For doing all of this. And all your help this week. It means...it means more than I can say. But I need to be alone tonight."

"Of course," Mom says. "Do you want us to take the boys home with us and give you some peace and quiet?"

If only she knew the quiet isn't so peaceful anymore. "No," I say quickly. "No, they should be here."

Mom nods, looking around. "Okay. Well, I'll just do the dishes and—"

"No." My voice is cracking and harsh, but I don't care. "No, everyone, just go, please. Please, just go." I'm going to lose it any second.

"Honey…" Daphne whispers, but it's Mom who puts a hand up and leads her from the room. I'm so grateful for my mom at that moment, who seems to sense what I need even when I'm not sure. She ushers my in-laws out of the room and gathers my father, leaving the house without another word, and when I'm alone in the living room, watching them drive away from the window, I sink to the floor.

I can't even make it into my bedroom before the sobs tear through me like ocean waves in a storm. I crumple into a ball, allowing the sadness to break out of the box I've kept it in and seep into my muscles and bones. My tendons and blood. Every ounce, every inch of me. Allowing myself to feel every shred of the rage, betrayal, confusion, and terrible sadness that I've repressed over the last few days.

I hate this.

I hate what this is turning me into. I hate that this is supposed to be a happy day, a day where we celebrate and spoil each other, and instead, I'm on my living room floor sobbing like a child.

I hate him.

I hate him.

I hate him.

How could he do this to me? Didn't he love me? Isn't he hurting, too?

And our children! How could he do this to our boys? The boys who look up to him and love him more than anyone on this planet?

When did we stop crying like this? Throwing ourselves on beds like petulant teenagers and letting out our rage? Dropping to the ground whenever the world got to be too much and just having a tantrum? I'm surprised by how good it makes me feel to release this pain without fear of judgment.

When I finally stop crying, my sobs turning silent and muscles aching from exertion, I hear a soft vibration from across the room. I sit up, rubbing my eyes with the backs of my hands as I listen closely.

I stand up from the ground and cross the room, grab my purse from the coffee table, and pull out my phone. I'm sure it's Mom checking in. For all I know, they didn't actually leave and have instead sat out in the driveway and listened to my entire meltdown.

But when I spot the words on the screen—**Unknown Caller**—my heart sinks. I don't want to do this again. I don't want to deal with whatever sick prank this is.

I answer the phone, but I don't say a word. Two can play this game. I just sit and let the seconds tick by, only the sound of my breathing filling the line.

Then, two words.

I swear my heart stops.

"Happy anniversary."

CHAPTER TWENTY-ONE

TATUM

Highland University
Twelve Years Ago

These assholes thought I was bluffing when I came back to campus, but they were wrong. *See if I care about spending Christmas away from all their bullshit.*

Mom will pick me. She will. She just needs a few days to come to her senses, and then she'll be begging me to come back. They're going to learn their place.

I jog across campus, bag in hand, and head for my dorm. I could've easily stayed at my parents' house while attending Highland, but I wanted the full college experience. I didn't want my mom breathing down my neck about every little thing. Besides, I wanted my foster brothers close by. I wanted to make sure they knew they were never going to escape me, not really.

When I spot her walking across campus, her arms

are loaded with books, her dark hair pulled back in a low ponytail. I have the sudden urge to wrap it around my fist and tug. The idea warms something deep in my stomach, and I jog after her, keeping back a fair distance until I can tell where she's going.

I watch her slip into her office, warmth and possibilities spreading through me. Once she's inside, I step in and shut the door behind me.

She spins around at the sound, obviously startled to see me. Her eyes flash wide, then shoot to the door as she takes a step back. "Mr. Thompson, I don't have office hours until after break. You'll have to come back."

"I'm not here for office hours," I say, stalking toward her. "I'm here for you." I step forward until we're just inches apart and reach my hand out, twirling a piece of loose hair near her ear around my finger.

She jerks back, swatting my hand away. "Excuse me? That's completely inappropriate. Do *not* touch me."

I lower my face to her ear, my breath tickling her skin, and she freezes. "I like it when you're feisty."

Snapping back to reality, she steps away again, huffing a breath. "As I said, I'm afraid you'll have to leave."

"Aww, come on, now. I've seen you naked. Don't you think we should even the score? It's only fair."

Her pretty cheeks flush pink, and she scowls at me. "Please, go, Mr. Thompson. This is inappropriate. I'll have to report it to the dean if you don't leave."

"I specialize in inappropriate, Professor. Haven't you heard?" I wiggle my brows at her, then turn and lean over her desk, blocking her in. "The dean is away for the break. Would you rather spank me instead? I like a little corporal punishment now and then. Just like I like when you call me Mr. Thompson." One corner of my lips tugs upward. "So formal. I'd like it even more if you were on your knees."

I see the fear flash in her eyes then, and it awakens something primal in me. I stand up straight again as she steps back, and I follow, pinning her between the desk and me. "This is inappropriate. You should leave."

"I will eventually," I promise, leaning in to kiss her mouth. "But not until I get to taste you."

She pulls back again, jerks back really, both hands on my chest. "Tatum, *stop.*" Her voice is firm, and it just turns me on more. She really thinks she's going to control me. It's sort of hot. I lean in and bite her neck. When she squeals, all the blood in my body shoots straight to my dick.

"Please go," she whispers, a hand lifting to the place on her neck that is now marred by an imprint of my teeth.

"I'm not finished yet."

"What do you want?" Her wide eyes meet mine. "He's your friend. Please don't do this."

"We're all alone, Professor." I lick my lips. "No one has to know."

"I would know." She tries to slip away from me, to

duck around me, but I catch her wrist, spinning her until her back slams into my chest. I rake a hand down her side, gripping her hip.

"Don't make me beg for it, Professor. I don't mind chasing what I want."

"Tatum, stop," she cries, pulling away, but I lock my hand around her wrist, the other on her hip even tighter. She can't move. "Stop or I'll scream."

"Scream, and I'll give you something to scream about." I spin her away from me and shove her into the wall, my body pressed to hers. Her scent is citrusy and fresh, and it consumes my thoughts. I close my eyes and inhale it, wondering what she must smell like everywhere. "We both know you want me. Why are we wasting our time?"

She doesn't say anything, just glares at me.

"On your knees," I order, tilting her chin up.

Her nostrils flare. "In your dreams."

"What would you know about my dreams, Professor?" I tease, licking along her jawbone. "On your knees, or I'll tell everyone you're sleeping with your students."

She holds eye contact, refusing to look afraid, though we can both feel her trembling. "So tell everyone. He's not my student, and we both know it."

"Then I'll send the whole school the photos you sent him." That stops her. She wavers, her eyes searching mine as I click my tongue. "You're a naughty girl, aren't you?"

"You're lying. Matteo would never show you those."

I bounce my head from side to side. "Eh, show me... leave his phone around so I could find them and send them to myself...what's the difference, really?" I pull my phone from my pocket, flipping through the photos I stole so she knows I'm not bluffing. "You do what I say, I'll delete them. If you don't, I'm happy to send them to everyone I know, your boss included. It's a shame to deprive them of the fun, really. These pictures have certainly provided me with"—my eyes flick up to meet hers—"hours of entertainment."

She swallows, and I catch the glint of tears in her eyes. When the first one falls, I lean forward and lick its path back up her cheek. This time, she doesn't move. She's as still as a stone.

I'm so hard it hurts, but I'm patient. I have to be. She wavers at the threat, I see it in her eyes, but eventually, her steely gaze returns. "Send them, then. It's illegal. If you want to go to jail, be my guest."

I smirk. "And if I tell them you asked me to send them? That you like messing around with students, and you wanted everyone to have them? I think we all know who they'll believe."

She locks her jaw. "That's a risk I'm willing to take."

I sigh. "Look, we can do this the easy way or the hard way. I'm not opposed to the hard way, but I think you'll find the easy way much more appealing."

"I'm not going to sleep with you, Tatum. No matter

what you say or do or how you threaten me. I'm with Matteo. I *love* Matteo."

I shrug one shoulder. "You can still be with Matteo. I don't want a wife, Professor. Just a good time." My hand lifts to her head, and I stroke that same piece of loose hair near her ear, wrapping the strand around my finger once more. Normally, girls look like shit when they wear their hair up, but somehow she manages to pull it off with flying colors.

"I'm sure there are plenty of other girls on campus who can help you out with that." She tries to slip away again, and I let her think she's going to, then grab her at the last second and shove her into the wall with more force than necessary. She cries out from the blow of it, and I press myself into her back, using the other hand to slide down her leg and lift the hem of her dress. Her skin is on fire as my fingers skate across it. When I reach the fabric of her underwear, I close my eyes and inhale the scent of her hair.

"I don't want other girls. I want you."

She struggles, but I don't give in. Her strength is no match for mine. I pull her back from the wall, tugging the front of her dress down, and snap a photo before she realizes what's happened. In it, we're both staring at the camera, her breasts entirely exposed. If you didn't know better, you might think we were a couple.

How fucking sweet.

She struggles to tug her dress back up, to cover herself with her one free hand, and I click my tongue.

"I guess I could just send this to Matteo instead. Break his *wittle* heart." I pucker out my bottom lip.

That causes her to go still as she turns to look at me. I drop her wrist, waiting.

"You and I both know he'd believe me if I said you came onto me," she says, bluffing. "If I said you assaulted me."

I scoff, looking away. "Like hell. Have you seen me? I don't need to assault anyone. Girls come to me." I step forward again, slipping my leg in between her thighs as I lower my voice. "They beg for me."

"He loves me." She swallows. "This will break him. Please don't do this. He's your friend."

"You're my friend," I mutter into her hair. She smells like absolute heaven. I nip at her ear, tracing the outside with my tongue. She shivers, sucking in a breath. I'm done waiting. "So be friendly." I shove her to the ground, and her knees hit the tile with a sharp smack. She cries out but doesn't give me the satisfaction of making more of a sound than she has to.

"No," she says, shaking her head.

"I'm not asking anymore." I unzip my pants and shove myself in her face, snapping a few more pictures with my phone. She realizes what I've done but is too slow to move. When her eyes meet mine, we both know I've won.

Her chin quivers as she locks eyes with mine, silently pleading.

"Do it, or I'll ruin his fucking life."

She swallows, her perfect little eyes meeting mine. "Please, Tatum."

I grab hold of her throat, squeezing until she can't take a breath. "Beg me again, ask me to stop again, and I'll bend you over this desk instead. And I promise I'm not as much of a gentleman as Matteo. *This* is the easy way. So make your choice." I release her neck, and she sucks in a deep breath.

She closes her eyes, a tear streaming down her cheek, and then she takes me in her hand and leans in, mouth open wide.

Fucking heaven.

CHAPTER TWENTY-TWO

CELINE

"Tate?" His voice is like a fever dream. It doesn't feel real. As much as I hate to admit it, even to myself, some huge part of me felt like I'd never hear it again.

Maybe I'm hallucinating. Maybe I'm imagining all of this. Maybe I really have had some sort of break-down. I'm not sure any of this is real.

"Tate? Is that you?"

I can only hear him breathing.

"Please. Please say something. Tell me something. Anything."

There's a long pause where I'm sure he's going to hang up, but then I hear, "I miss you." His voice is soft and slow, like he's trying not to be heard, and it reminds me of talking on the phone long after curfew when I was a teenager, covers pulled over my head.

"It's really you." My voice cracks. "I can't believe it. I

miss you too. So much. Where are you? What is happening?"

"I'm sorry," he whispers.

"Sorry?"

Once again he doesn't say anything, leaving me in silence as I listen to the sound of his breathing.

"I know about the money."

Again, there's nothing.

"The boys miss you, Tate. Please just…if not for me, will you come back for them? At least to say goodbye?" I hate that I'm crying right now. Hate that I'm begging. "I don't understand. I thought things were okay, and I don't know why you left or what I did wrong, but I miss you. I really miss you, and I want you here. I want you to hold me and tell me it's going to be okay and that this is all a misunderstanding. The boys miss you so much, Tate. They miss their daddy." I sink to the floor, wrapping my arms around myself. "Please say something."

"I can't."

"Where are you?"

"I can't tell you that."

"Why?"

Nothing.

I rock back and forth, scrubbing my hand over my arm. "The police are looking for you. What am I supposed to tell them?"

"You can't tell them anything."

"Why?" I demand, my voice indignant.

"Because I said."

"Tate."

"I have to go."

"I know about the professor. In college." I brace myself for the line to click, for the call to end, and when it doesn't, I go on. "Aubrey Vance. I know all of your friends are dying, and…I think you know why it's happening."

I wait for him to deny it, but he doesn't.

"Tate, please. Why did you take the money? What is happening?"

"I fucked up, okay?" His voice cracks. "I ruined everything."

My chest splits open. *He's talking. He's finally talking.* "What do you mean? What did you do? Whatever it is, we can get through this. I promise you, we just—"

"No. I have to go."

Ice-cold panic seizes me. "No. What? Why? Please don't hang up. Please don't leave me like this."

"I'll call back when I can, okay?"

"No. No, that's not good enough. Tell me something. Just give me something. You can trust me."

"Don't trust anyone," he blurts out. "Don't tell anyone I called. Don't tell anyone what you know, especially not about…about that."

"About the professor?"

"Don't say it again, Celine. I mean it."

"Why?"

"Just trust me, okay? I'll explain this all when I can. I

know you think you know things now, know who I was, but I'm not that person anymore. I've changed. You changed me." His voice grows softer. "I'm sorry, I have to go."

With that, the line goes dead, and I'm left alone in the silence.

CHAPTER TWENTY-THREE

TATUM

Twelve Years Ago

Just like I suspected, it doesn't take long for them to all come crawling back to me. Exactly one day goes by before I hear from them.

It's Dakota first, of course.

I answer the call and don't say anything. We just sit in silence. *Wait 'em out. Let 'em sweat.*

"Tatum, I know you're there."

My brothers are used to this sort of treatment, but only when they deserve it. Which, to be fair, is often.

"Listen, dude, your mom is really upset. I know you're pissed at us, but don't take it out on her. Just... just come home, okay? If you want us to leave, we will. But just come home and make up with her. It's Christmas. She shouldn't be sad."

"Why should I?"

"Because she's your mom."

"And? Doesn't give her the right to treat me like shit."

Dakota sucks in a breath. "You're right. But maybe, just this once, you could let it go. Like a gift to her."

I suck my front teeth, thinking. "Yeah, okay. I guess I will."

"Yeah?" He didn't think it would be this easy, but I'm bored here now that I've gotten what I wanted. I'd rather be home in my own bed than in this stupid dorm.

"Yeah, what the hell, why not?" Without another word, I hang up and start gathering my things. I can't wait to tell the boys about the Christmas gift I gave myself.

Back at home, everyone walks on eggshells around me just trying to keep me happy, but I'm on my best behavior. I don't apologize, but I also don't make them apologize to me. I hug Mom and pretend everything is peachy, just biding my time.

When Christmas morning rolls around, we all exchange presents, and I give everyone their gift except for Matteo. Nice gifts, too. Expensive ones, while they just give me cheap shit.

Mom buys us all a ton of clothes, but I'm the only one who gets Xbox games too, which is fine by me.

Matteo doesn't say anything about the fact that I skipped right over him when I was passing out my gifts. No one does, in fact, but I can tell they've all noticed. The guys slip on their watches from me. They have lion emblems engraved on their undersides to match the tattoos we got. I told them it was to symbolize our brotherhood, our pride.

We've known each other since we were young—three and four years old, and all staying in the same foster home. We were split up a few different times, but we always ended up back together like it was some kind of sign. More likely because there were only a few homes that would take teenagers; even fewer that would take rowdy teenagers who were always getting into trouble. And then Lane and Daphne took me in, and a year later, I was adopted. I thought I'd never have to see my brothers again, and then I did when we all agreed to go to the same college. I decided it couldn't hurt to have people around who would do anything for me.

Then, freshman year, I got tired of looking at the burn scars on my shoulder from one of the deadbeat foster dads and got a tattoo to cover them up. Shocked the shit out of me when they got them out of solidarity.

At least that's what they said. They probably just wanted to copy me again.

After presents, while Mom and Dad are putting out Christmas breakfast, I find Matteo in his bedroom getting dressed and toss the watch box at him. He stares at it with an odd expression and, once his shirt is down over his head, picks it up.

"Didn't think I forgot about you, did you?"

"Wasn't sure," he says simply. Matteo's always been the one to give me trouble. If anyone was going to argue with me or attempt to stand up to me, it was him, but I'm about to put him in his place once and for all.

"I got ya something. I just thought you might want to open it up in private. In case you get all weepy and shit."

"Thanks," he says, tucking it into his pocket.

"Aren't you going to open it?" I ask, dropping down on his bed.

"I thought you just said I should open it in private."

"I meant not in front of everyone else. You can open it now, though, and you should."

His hand taps his pocket. "Why?"

"Because it's the polite thing to do," I remind him. "And you're mister manners, aren't you?"

He wants to roll his eyes or argue. I can see it. I think he's physically fighting against rolling his eyes, in fact, but he doesn't. He's going to keep the peace at all costs.

At least until he sees what I got him.

I swallow, watching as he pulls the watch box from his pocket. My pulse is pounding as I wait.

He senses that something is up, and I know he doesn't want to open it, but he also has no choice.

That's the beauty of it. I have all the power, always have.

Slowly, he opens the watch box. His expression changes as he processes what he's seeing. He drops the box on the comforter, holding the crumpled photographs in his hands as he unfolds them. When he realizes what I've given him, he shoves them into his pockets and steps toward me.

"What the actual fuck?"

I grin without my teeth. "Are you surprised? Really? I wanted her. You knew I wanted her. Turns out, she wanted me just as bad." I whistle. "She's insatiable, bro. No wonder you were trying to keep her for yourself."

"You fucking asshole!" He launches himself at me, but I stand up, still as stone, and it stops him in his tracks.

"Watch it, because if you lay a single finger on me, if you even think of breathing a word of this to anyone..." A wicked smile crosses my lips as my gaze flicks down to the pictures he's tucked away in his pocket. "Let's just say those aren't the only copies in existence, and I'm more than happy to share. Whether or not you take her class, I do, and I don't think the dean would be too happy about one of his professors fraternizing with students, do you?"

"Are you threatening me?"

I click my tongue and wiggle my finger at him. "*Promising*. Better word. But don't worry, I've gotten what I wanted. You can have her back now."

"She's not a toy," he cries, his eyes filling with tears. *My god, how pathetic. He's seriously going to cry over this? What a loser.*

"Could've fooled me. She was a lot of fun to play with. So much more exciting than blocks."

His hands ball into fists again, and though we both know he wants to kill me, he can't touch me. He never could.

"Shouldn't have sent me back to campus, Mafia Matteo. That's on you. What did you think was going to happen? Surely you knew she was there. I mean, you can't blame her really. She saw what she wanted and went after it. Why would she want you when she could have me?"

"What's going on in here?" Dakota appears in the doorway, and I jerk my head around to see him. I slide my arm around Matteo's shoulders, and my hand plants right on his collarbone, applying just enough pressure that he tenses.

"Nothing at all. Right, Matteo?" He's silent for a long while, and I squeeze his shoulder again, this time harder. "Unless there's something you need to tell the class?"

He jerks his shoulder away from me. "Fuck off."

I beam. "Same old Mafia Matteo."

CHAPTER TWENTY-FOUR

CELINE

Two days go by as I sit in radio silence, not totally sure the entire phone call wasn't a dream. If it wasn't for the call in my call log, I could easily be convinced I imagined the whole thing. I spend the next two miserable days filled with stress and sweating and random crying fits. Two days where I plaster on a smile in front of the boys and a stoic face in front of my parents and pretend I'm still just holding on.

I haven't gotten any new updates from the police, and I'm afraid to reach out to them because I'm terrified I'll slip up and somehow let them know I spoke with him. Maybe I should. Some part of me worries that he only called because he found out I'd closed our bank accounts. Maybe he never thought I'd actually go through with it. Maybe he expected me to be the trusting, doting wife, sitting around waiting for him to return like he was coming home from war, rather than abandoning us.

Maybe he wouldn't actually be wrong to think that because here I sit. In bed at the end of a long day, staring at the phone until my eyes are so dry I have to blink. Maybe he knows me all too well.

Every time my phone goes off, I jump up like it's him. I want to hear from him like I want to live. No matter what he's done, I can't make myself be mad at him. I want to trust him, want to believe there could be some sort of explanation.

So when the phone finally goes off after two long days of waiting in silence, and those two words appear on my screen—**Unknown Caller**—my heart leaps into my throat as if I'm a teenager waiting for my crush to call.

I swipe my finger across the screen before the first ring has ended. "Tate?"'

"I have a plan."

"A plan." I repeat the words. "What do you mean?"

"I'm going to come home."

"Okay." It's a kick to the chest I don't understand. He's coming home just like that? Like he just woke up and decided? Has he been able to come home all this time? "When? Now?"

"No. Tomorrow. I'll come home tomorrow night."

I sink. "Tomorrow night? Okay. Why…night? And why not tonight? Why do you have to wait?" I'm mumbling, processing. He sounds so calm, so sure of himself. I hate it, especially when I sound like a bumbling mess.

"I'll explain it all when I get there."

"But why can't you explain it now?"

He doesn't answer, allowing the silence to worry me again.

"Okay, fine, tomorrow. Are you…are you safe? Will you at least tell me that?"

"I'm safe. I'm okay," he says. "I'll be better when I'm home."

"We miss you so much."

He clears his throat. "I need you to do me a favor, though."

"Okay. Anything." I'm pathetic.

"Have you told anyone that we've spoken?"

"No, of course not. You asked me not to."

"Good. Okay. Keep the secret for another day for me, okay? And do you think you could get your mom to watch the boys tomorrow night?"

"Here? Where are we going?"

"No. Have her take them to their house. When I come home, we need to be alone."

Chills line my skin. "Alone. But why? They miss you. They'll be so excited you're home. I want to tell them."

"I know. I know. We just need one night together, just us, so I can explain everything."

"But I don't understand. Explain it now and then come home."

"I can't. You'll understand soon, I promise." His voice is cold and empty. I've never been afraid of my husband, but suddenly I am.

"Can you just tell me something now? Anything? You're scaring me."

"I'll see you tomorrow."

"Tate, please—"

He ends the call, and I'm alone again, left to ponder what exactly just happened. Tate is coming home, so why don't I feel relieved about it?

CHAPTER TWENTY-FIVE

TATUM

Highland University
Twelve Years Ago

When we get back to campus after break, the first thing I do is plan a party. Senior year is going out with a bang if I have anything to say about it—and I do. I have everything to say about it.

Matteo hasn't spoken to me since Christmas, but he'll be there because I told him to be. They all know better than to cross me.

When the night of the party rolls around, people are already toasted before I arrive with the boys.

"Where's Matteo?" Dakota asks, and I swear to god these two must be in love because if this motherfucker asks me about our dumbass friend one more time—

"He'll be here."

"Go unload our car," Bradley tells one of the few underclassmen we invited, patting him on the shoulder.

"Sure thing, boss." The boy jumps up without question, rushing toward the parking lot where my car waits, filled with alcohol I scored earlier.

"Are you sure about this?" Dakota asks, pulling me aside. "It feels extreme."

"Are you questioning me?"

"I'm just saying that Matteo is our friend. I don't know what's up with him lately, but embarrassing him in front of everyone isn't cool."

"Oh? I didn't realize you'd had a change of heart, madam." I clutch my hands to my chest like a little housewife on the prairie. Then I drop them, glaring at him. "Maybe you'd rather I embarrassed *you* in his place."

His jaw twitches. "It doesn't have to be like this, Tatum. We all know it. We used to have fun, you know? What happened to those days?"

"Oh, right. Gee, I forgot. It was so much fun when our foster dad twisted my arm just to see how long it would take until it broke." I fake a laugh. "Wasn't that a blast?"

He rolls his eyes.

"Oh! Oh! And what about the time…yeah, maybe you were talking about the time he burned the shit out of my shoulder for letting you go outside during the summer when we weren't supposed to leave the house. What about all the fun we had that day?"

"Point made, dude," he grumbles.

"No, I want to know. Was that the fun you meant? Or was it when they used to film us and sell it to fucking pedos on the internet? Wasn't that shit fun? Some of my best memories, personally. The really heartfelt stuff that you embroider on pillows and put in a scrapbook." I wrinkle my chin with mock nostalgia. "Or what about the other houses, like the one where they'd lock us in our rooms without dinner? Or make us clean their fucking houses like we were little government-provided servants. Tell me more about all the fun we had, Dakota. I'm having trouble remembering it all, and I really don't want to forget a thing."

"I get it," he grumbles, eyes distant. "Enough."

I jab my finger into his chest. "I was the one who protected you back then, wasn't I?"

His Adam's apple bobs.

"Wasn't I?"

"Yes, of course you were."

"And we made a pact back then to stick together, didn't we?"

"Yes."

Again, I stab him in the chest with my finger. This time it's so hard he winces. "Then we stick together, plain and simple."

He nods, but he doesn't say anything as his eyes find something over my shoulder. "He's here."

I turn around to see Matteo standing just behind me. He looks ready to kill me, which is a surprising turn of events given how long he's had to calm down. I expected him to have come crawling back by now, but I have to admire his strength to hold out. I wave for the boys to follow me and lead them into the woods to our usual spot.

Whether they want to or not, they do exactly as I say, stopping only when I stop. I tease them, stopping abruptly, then taking giant steps and then short, quick ones, and they follow suit, growing more annoyed by the minute. They really do make this too easy.

Finally, when we've reached the clearing where we have our bonfires, I turn around, holding up a hand that tells them to listen.

"I think some of you have forgotten who I am. Am I not the brother who protected you all those years? Am I not the brother who took countless beatings for each and every one of you? Am I not the one who made sure the bullies didn't pick on you when your clothes smelled like ass and were two sizes too small?"

There are a few mumbles of acknowledgment, but it's not enough.

"Am I *not?*" I shout, my voice echoing through the woods, though not loud enough to be heard over the blaring music at the party.

"Yes," they all chime in, voices in unison.

I blink rapidly. "Then *perhaps* someone wants to tell me why the fuck I've been getting so much resistance."

I narrow my gaze at them, pointing at each individual one. "Because I thought the deal was that I say, 'Jump,' and you say, 'How high?'" I cock a brow, then cross my arms. "Let's test it, shall we? Jump."

They exchange looks, and I bellow, "*Jump!*"

Two of them jump and the others ask, "How high?" *Fucking idiots.*

I widen my stance, staring them down. "I thought the deal was that I tell you to take my test or give me your sweatshirt or wash my car or fucking wipe my hairy ass, and you do it. Have I been wrong about that?"

They scowl, looking at each other.

"We're your friends, Tatum. Your brothers. But we aren't your servants," Bradley says softly. "We will fight for you. Die for you. But the way you've been acting is..." His voice goes soft, and I don't hear whatever word he's saying as I stalk toward him.

"Is what?" I demand.

He doesn't meet my eyes.

"Is what?" I shout.

He looks up finally. "Unhinged, bro. You're scaring us."

I stare at him for a long time, letting several uncomfortable seconds pass before I step back and scan each of their faces, waiting for someone to step in and defend me, to tell him he's wrong. "Is that how you all feel?" I demand.

No one agrees with him, at least not aloud, but they don't disagree either.

"I'm in charge," I say firmly. "I say, 'Run.' You say, 'Where?' I say, 'Hide.' You don't come out until I tell you you can. I say, 'My car needs gas.' You say, 'I've got it.'" I turn and look at Matteo, my eyes drilling into him. "I say, 'I want to fuck your girl.' You say, 'Have at it.' You hand me the fucking condom. Hell, maybe you even put it on. Am I making myself clear?"

Every other head turns to look at Matteo, but his eyes are locked on mine.

"And before any of you even thinks about arguing, let me remind you that I have enough dirt on all of you to take you down ten times over. Videos. Photos. You will do as I say, or your lives are over. Is that understood?"

The boys stare at me with rage in their eyes. It fuels me like nothing I've ever felt. My entire body feels electric, like lightning. I'm shaking with adrenaline and spite.

"No?" I dig in my ear, pretending to clean it out because I obviously couldn't hear their enthusiastic agreement, then grab my phone, opening it to my videos. I scroll back a few months and hold it out to Aaron. "Remember when you got so drunk you tried to suck your own—"

"Stop!" he shouts, covering his eyes. "I'm with you, okay? I'm with you, dude."

"We're all with you," Bradley says. "You don't have to do this."

"Good," I say when I spot the woman walking toward us through the woods, her pretty black hair pulled up in a ponytail again, bag clutched to her chest. I'm hard already. "Because things are about to get a whole lot more interesting."

CHAPTER TWENTY-SIX

CELINE

When I wake up the next morning, there's a sense of peace settled over me that I haven't felt in a long time.

For once, I have an answer about Tate. I don't know where he is or what has happened, but I know he's alive. I know he's coming home to me, even if it won't be to give me the answer I'm hoping for. Even if it won't be to tell me this has all been a misunderstanding, and he never wanted to leave and only took all our money so he could put it in a better investment account he just hadn't had the chance to tell me about yet, at least I will know. And knowing is always better than wondering. If I know, I can move forward. I can choose strength.

As of right now, the only thing I can do is try to understand what feels impossible to understand.

The house is still quiet, which takes me by surprise until I realize that it's nine a.m., and my parents must've already taken the boys to school. They let me sleep in, and for the first time, I was actually able to. It makes me sad I didn't say goodbye to the boys and wish them a good day, but I'll make it up to them as soon as Tate is home safe. Maybe I'll even make a cake —or, let's be honest, *buy* a cake.

I wash my face and brush my teeth, running a comb through my curls before tying them up off of my neck. I'm starting to feel better already. More normal. No one prepares you for how quickly that happens, how quickly an unthinkable reality becomes normal.

But it's almost over. Just one more day. Less than a day, really.

In the hall, I pop my head into the boys' rooms to make sure they're both gone, and when I'm positive they are, I text my mom to say thank you and make my way into the kitchen to make a cup of coffee. I can't believe how much I've missed the silence. I guess I didn't realize it until right now, but the entire house has been buzzing lately with concern and expectations. My parents and in-laws are well-meaning, of course, and I can't fault them or say I wish they'd do anything differently, it's just nice to have a few moments of silence for the first time in a while. To be able to feel what I'm feeling without an audience.

In a sort of cruel irony, a knock on the door interrupts my thoughts. My chest tightens, blood running cold.

Is he here already?

He said he'd be coming tonight, not today, right? Or was I just so tired and distraught I'd misunderstood? I run a hand over my hair and hurry toward the door, hoping the knock won't wake up the boys. Then I remember they're already at school for the day. *Gosh, my mind is so frazzled.*

When I reach the door, my heart sinks, then tenses again. It's not Tate, but it is the police. I can't tell them anything, can't let them know I've spoken to Tate, but I'm not a good liar. Especially not to the police. I'm going to totally fail at this.

I swing open the door to see Detective Monroe waiting on our porch. He smiles without showing his teeth. "Good morning, Mrs. Thompson."

"Good morning. Is everything alright?" *Do they know I spoke with Tate? Do they know I'm lying? Have they bugged the house? Are they listening to me? Following me?*

"Yes, I just wanted to bring this by while I was out on another call today. They were going to reach out to you about coming to pick it up, but I was in the area." He reaches into his jacket pocket and pulls out a plastic bag. Inside are Tate's cell phone and wallet.

I suck in a breath when he places the entire bag into my hands. There's writing on the outside. Tate's name, a date, and more that I don't understand. "I get these back?"

"Yep. Our IT team has run the phone through all of their systems and pulled the information they needed, so they're all yours again." He pats the doorframe. "Do you have any updates for me?"

It feels like a test. I feel like he knows the answer, and I'm about to fail. "Um, no. I don't think so." My entire body is a block of ice as I wait for him to respond.

He waits for several seconds but eventually nods. "Okay. Well, you know how to reach me if anything comes up. Take care of yourself, yeah?" He takes a step back, pulling his sunglasses down over his eyes before he turns around and heads toward the car.

In the kitchen, I cut the bag open and flip Tate's phone over in my hand, pressing the button to turn it on. The screen stays dark. I should've known it wouldn't be that easy. Of course his phone is dead at this point. I open the junk drawer and pull out an old phone charger, plugging it in with shaking hands and tapping the counter as I wait for the device to come on.

When it eventually does, a photo of the four of us at the petting zoo fills the screen, and my throat goes tight.

What if Tate doesn't want this anymore? What if he doesn't want us?

It's a hard reality to consider, that this man isn't who he swore to me he was. There were no signs that he was unhappy from what I can recall. He seemed as in love as I am. He was an attentive and present husband and father. A true partner. He never forgot a birthday or anniversary. He loved us and took care of us.

Was it all just a con? A trick?

On the phone, he said I'd changed him. Fixed him. Was that all a lie?

The only sign that there was ever anything wrong was...the text.

Tell her.

I open his text messages, wondering if it will still be there. To my surprise, it is. A number not saved in his contacts and a single message. Surely the police looked into this. They must already know who it is that sent it.

My thumb hovers over the screen for several seconds. What's the worst that can happen? If it's about work, I'll just apologize and move on. But if it's not...

Has Tate left me for another woman?

Does this number belong to that woman?

The curiosity is too much to bear. I select the number and place the phone to my ear.

"I wondered when you'd call." The voice on the phone belongs to a man, and it's one I recognize, but it takes me a few seconds to place it. "Your wife came by the other day."

"Aaron."

His voice comes out in a breathless whisper, and I know I've ruined it. I just know he's going to hang up on me, but he doesn't. "Who is this?"

I lick my lips, trying to pull myself together. "It's

Celine Thompson. Tate's wife. I just got his phone back from the police."

"Oh. I just assumed he had finally resurfaced."

"No, still nothing," I lie. "I saw the text on his phone. You told him to 'tell her.' Were you talking about me? What did you want him to tell me? Tate said it was something about a bad appraisal at work, but I'm guessing that was a lie."

He huffs a breath.

"Please just tell me. Is Tate lying to me? Did he leave me? I know you don't know me, and you don't owe me anything, but please…if you know something, just tell me the truth. All I want is to know the truth so I can move on."

"I, um, look, I can't talk about this over the phone. Can you meet me somewhere?"

"At your work?"

"No, not here. There's a restaurant near here. It's quiet. We'll be able to talk. I'll send you the address. Meet me at…" He pauses. "Meet me at one, okay?"

"Yeah, sure. Okay. And thank you."

"I don't know if you'll be saying thank you after I tell you everything," he grumbles. "I'll see you soon. Oh, and obviously, don't tell anyone we're meeting."

Before I can respond, he ends the call and I stare down at the screen.

One step closer to understanding the truth.

CHAPTER TWENTY-SEVEN

TATUM

Highland University
Twelve Years Ago

When Professor Vance walks out of the treeline so we can see her, everyone stiffens. They're wondering how much she heard of what we just said, but they have bigger problems.

"Gentlemen, our guest of honor has arrived," I say, holding out a hand toward her.

She's confused, understandably, and her gaze falls to Matteo. "I thought I was coming to meet you. He texted me and said he wanted to help fix this, that he wanted us to talk." Her eyes are red and bloodshot, as are his. "What is this?"

Matteo's jaw locks. "Ask him."

She spins around to me. "What can you possibly want from me? Haven't you done enough?"

I cock my head to the side. "Actually, I think it was you who did most of the work, don't you? I can't possibly take all the credit."

Out of the corner of my eye, I see Matteo's hands ball into fists.

Aubrey's shoulders crumple inward, and her eyes fill with tears. "You ruined everything."

Matteo walks forward, gathering her in his arms, and it would be the perfect little Hallmark moment if it wasn't pathetic. I walk forward, jerking them apart. "Moment's over."

"Leave her alone, Tatum," Matteo growls. "Let her go. If you want to hurt someone, hurt me. Take whatever this is out on me, but let her go. She's not part of this."

I grin because he couldn't be more wrong. "Oh, actually, she's the entire part of this. The most important part."

"Let her go, man," he begs. This time *he actually begs*, but I'm not listening.

"Come on." I wave them forward, closer to the ashy pit where we have our bonfires. When I turn back and find I'm not being followed, I tap my phone. "Unless I need to send a few emails."

Bradley and Aaron step forward first, then Dakota, but Matteo and Aubrey stay in place.

"Make sure they come with us," I order. "If not willingly, drag them." They exchange looks, but eventually the guys grab Matteo first, then Aubrey, and push them forward. They don't look happy about it, but I don't need them to be happy. I need them to follow orders.

Matteo digs his feet into the ground, trying to stop them, but he's silent. Angry. He's also no match on strength against Dakota and Bradley.

I lead them to the firepit. "Get a fire going," I tell Dakota, then look at Bradley and Aaron. "You two, keep them still."

Everyone is growing restless. If I don't act quickly, I'm going to lose them, but tonight will show them why they've always been afraid to mess with me. After tonight, there will be no doubt who is in charge here.

"Let us go," Aubrey argues, jerking her arm and trying to get free of Aaron's grasp.

"I'm sorry," he mutters. "I can't."

She addresses me then, eyes made of pure lava, words dripping venom. "I'm here, aren't I? I'm not going anywhere without Matteo, okay? So you've got me. Just let me go. We're not animals."

I ignore her as I watch Dakota building the fire, then bend down and reach into my bag, digging around. I wasn't sure what I'd need tonight to pull this off, but if all goes as planned, I won't have to touch the knife or any of the more dangerous stuff. I pull out the roll of duct tape and toss a lighter to Dakota.

"What is that for?" Matteo asks, eyeing the tape as he finally jerks free of Bradley's grasp and moves toward me with his hands up.

After snapping out of his apparent stupor, Bradley

scurries to catch up with him, pulling him back. "Chill, man," he says, keeping his voice low. "Just let him calm down."

"I want to know what he's going to do," Matteo says, eyes on me.

"Watch and find out," I tease, winking at Aubrey as I take her arm and force her to drop her bag onto the ground, kicking it aside. "Now, if you're a good girl, nothing bad has to happen here tonight, okay? So play nice."

"Let her go," Matteo begs, trying to fight his way free. Bradley looks conflicted, but no one challenges me. They all do exactly as I've asked.

"Hold him still," I warn Bradley, pulling Aubrey away from them and nodding for Aaron to help Bradley hold Matteo. Matteo is strong, but with both boys holding onto him, he stands no chance. I lead Aubrey to one of the wooden chairs we've placed around the firepit and set her down gently. Her eyes are laced with fear and fury as I place her hands on the chair arms and tear off a piece of duct tape with my teeth.

I secure her arms, taping them in place, then move on to her legs. Every eye is on me, waiting to see what I'll do next. She keeps looking at them, waiting for them to save her, but they won't. They're cowards at the end of the day, and loyal to a fault.

She was wrong when she said we aren't animals. We are. We always have been. To pretend to be anything but an animal is to wear a mask all day and night, but out here, this is where my mask can finally come off. There are no consequences here. No rules.

Once she's completely secured and unable to escape, I walk back to my bag and bend down, reaching inside of it with purposeful sluggishness, making them wait to see what I'll do next. Aubrey struggles against the tape holding her in place, but the attempt is feeble. She isn't giving it her all. She knows it's no use.

I pull the bottle of vodka and a few shot glasses out of my bag, holding them up in the air. "Jesus, you all look like I'm going to pull a bomb out of my bag or something. It's just some spirits to get the festivities going. Calm down, you bunch of lunatics." I gather the plastic shot glasses and pass them out, pouring a shot for everyone except Aubrey.

"Well, what are you waiting for?" I down mine. "Take a shot, pussies."

Slowly, they all do, and with the fire started, I feel heat inside and outside, burning for power. My heart beats like a drum of war, letting me know this is right. This is what leaders do. This is how they prove what they're worth, who they are.

When I approach Aubrey, I run my tongue over my teeth, examining her. "Hmm, I guess you can't really hold a shot glass like this, can you?" I glance at the bottle, a wicked idea forming in my mind. "Open."

She stares at me, a hint of defiance in her eyes, and I hold the bottle close to her face.

"Open," I tell her through gritted teeth.

Slowly, her lips part, eyes locked on me.

I chuckle, making her wait. "I've seen this some-where before." Lifting the bottle away from her mouth, I pour the shot into my own mouth instead, then lean forward and spit the liquid into hers.

She spits the shot out in surprise, spewing it all over me, herself, and the grass.

I wipe a hand over my doused shirt. "Oh, ho, ho." I laugh. "You really shouldn't have done that."

"Leave her the fuck alone, Tate," Matteo bellows. "It's me you're mad at. Punish me. Let her go. Come on, man. Please. Please let her go."

"I'll get to you later," I say without looking his way. "Now, Professor, open up. Again, please."

Her eyes flick to Matteo.

"Don't look at him. Look at me."

Slowly, she does what she's told, opening her mouth wide. "Good girl," I purr, filling my mouth with vodka and lowering it to hers. I do it at a snail's pace this time, letting my lips touch hers gently before I spit the liquid into her mouth. She swallows, and I kiss her, demanding more, tilting her head back as I let my tongue explore. Once I've licked the taste from every square inch of her mouth, I pull back, not wanting to, but needing to, and wipe my lips with a satisfied hum. I have to pace myself. Being a leader is about self-control as much as it is controlling the rest of them. "Deli-cious." I lift the bottle toward my mouth. "Again."

She shakes her head, her brows drawing together. *"Again."*

Trembling, her mouth opens again, but less wide this time. She looks scared as I pour the vodka into my mouth, then swish it around. I lean forward, never taking my eyes off of hers. Hovering just above her open mouth, I spit the alcohol out slowly, emptying it inside of her. My heart pounds, cheeks flush. I've never experienced anything so hot.

A bit of vodka spills out onto her chin and down her neck when she swallows, and I lower my mouth to her collarbone, running my tongue across her skin, lapping the liquor up. Her throat pulses as she swallows again, and I trace her jawbone with my teeth. "What a good girl you are, Professor. *My* good girl, aren't you?"

"Come on, man," Matteo says, and I'm nearly sure he's crying over there. "Please, stop this."

"Do you want me to stop?" I demand, holding my hands up.

He nods.

"Really? You want me to stop? Because I thought you'd want a few drinks in all of our systems before what comes next, but if you're already ready to move on, then I'm happy to oblige."

Even in the light of the fire, I see his face pale. "Please don't hurt her. I'll do whatever you want. Just don't hurt her."

I grin, grabbing hold of her hair and tilting her head

back, pouring the remaining contents of the vodka bottle into her mouth and all over her face as she struggles and screams and tries to get away.

Matteo bellows like an animal, fighting them with all of his might.

"Hold him back!" I warn the guys.

When I run out of vodka, she's gasping for breath, her hair and clothing drenched in the alcohol. Her chest shines in the firelight, rising and falling with every panicked inhale or exhale. It's as if she can't get the oxygen into her lungs fast enough.

I drop the bottle on the ground, and our eyes meet. Nothing exists in this moment except the two of us. She wants me, even if she doesn't know it yet. More importantly, I want her.

"Now"—I hold up a finger toward Matteo, still looking only at Aubrey—"here's what's going to happen. I'm going to let your girl suck my cock, and you're going to watch it. And you're not going to say a *single fucking word*, and you're not going to look away, do you hear me? You're going to watch her worship me. You're going to watch this hungry girl drain every last drop like it's your favorite television show. Because if you…if you so much as blink your goddamn eyes, I'm going to make sure she spends the rest of the night on her back taking every single one of the rest of us in every hole she has. I'm going to make you listen while she shouts every one of your friends' names, while she begs us for more, do you hear me? You won't leave this fucking place without that image scarred into your mind, I promise you."

Her eyes are wide with fear as I start unbuttoning my pants. "Just like last time, baby," I whisper, grabbing hold of the back of her head and jerking her forward until her lips graze me. "You've got it. Show him how good you are for me. Be loud, baby girl, okay? I want him to hear how much you love my dick."

She closes her eyes, tears streaming down her cheeks as her mouth opens and her lips wrap around me. "Eyes open," I warn her as she slides down my length.

On command, she opens her eyes. I look up at the sky and scream, power coursing through my veins. I'm unstoppable. All powerful. I am a fucking god.

Then: *pain.*

Pain like I've never felt before.

Pain that tears your eyes from their sockets and peels your skin from your body. I rip my head down, looking at where she's attached to me, her teeth locked onto me, biting down. In her eyes, there is a challenge. If I pull away, she's going to rip it off.

I shout and scream and punch her in the face, but she doesn't let up. *I'm going to kill her.*

CHAPTER TWENTY-EIGHT

CELINE

With the boys at school, once I get ready, I immediately head for the restaurant Aaron suggested we meet at. Reggie's is a small, run-down diner that somehow manages to look both Western and regal.

From the parking lot, I text my phone from Tate's and give Aaron's name and the address of the place we're meeting. I don't think I'm in danger, but I have to be careful. If anything happens, I want someone to know where I was and who I was with, but I don't want to alarm my parents if nothing bad is going to happen.

Inside, there's a sign that instructs us to seat ourselves, so I find a booth and take a seat. When the waitress comes over, dressed in denim from head to toe, I order a coffee and scan the restaurant for any sign of Aaron.

The place is quiet, but they have Dolly Parton's "I Will Always Love You" crooning through the speakers, which will make it easier to have a private conversation. I watch the door like a hawk, studying the parking lot for any sign of him, but there is none. He's not here.

When he's fifteen minutes late, I start to worry I've been stood up. But why? Why would he want me to come here? What good would it do? Did he chicken out? Has he decided not to help me after all?

After thirty minutes, I try to call him from Tate's phone, but he doesn't pick up, and I have to accept that this was a waste of time. It makes me angrier now, perhaps more than ever before, to have my time wasted. Maybe because I understand how precious time is. Perhaps because I made my parents pick the boys up from school on a day they didn't have to, perhaps because I'm missing precious time with my boys when I feel like I haven't seen them much at all lately, when they need me more than ever.

Either way, when the waitress comes back around, I ask her for the check with a bitter resentment burning in my chest. As I'm grabbing my card from my wallet, the restaurant door opens once more, and I look up.

Aaron scans the restaurant, the skin around his eyes wrinkling as he searches for me. A hint of recognition flashes across his expression when his gaze hits my face. It takes him a few seconds to be sure it's me, and I wave at him before he starts walking my way.

When he reaches the booth, he slips down across from me. "Sorry I'm late. I got held up in traffic."

I glance out at the empty street skeptically, but he doesn't bother trying to sell the lie more than that.

"Well, thank you for meeting me," I say softly. "I really appreciate it."

He opens his mouth to respond, but before he can say anything, the waitress is back to take his order. Looking over the menu quickly, he orders a Diet Coke and a tuna sandwich with onion rings, and when she disappears, he folds his hands in front of himself on the table. "Truth be told, I almost didn't come."

I nod, having assumed as much.

"I don't like to talk badly about my friends. More than that, I don't like to talk about what happened between us back then, or to tell my friends' secrets, but if it will help you find Tate, you have a right to know the truth. Because I do want him to be found. I hope more than anything that he is."

I don't know what has suddenly made him decide to help me, and I don't care. I just need his help. "I want that too, which is why I need you to tell me everything you know. Starting with the text message. It was about me, then? You wanted Tate to tell me something, right?"

He huffs out a breath through his nose. "No. The text message was about…" He pauses when his food arrives, thanking the waitress, then takes a sip of his drink before he begins talking again. "It was about Tate's mom."

"Daphne."

He nods. "She was always Mrs. T to us. I wanted him to tell her that one of our friends, Bradley, was going to tell someone our secret. Something happened years ago, and we all swore we'd never talk about it, but he was going to break our pact. I wanted Tate to tell Mrs. T before that happened."

"But what happened? What was the secret? Was this in college?"

He nods, taking the bread off of his sandwich to examine the meat and setting it back in place, smashing the bread down. I think he's avoiding meeting my eyes. "We were kids. It's no excuse, but we were stupid kids. We grew up together in foster care, the five of us."

"You, Tate, Bradley Jennings, Dakota Miller, and Matteo Acri."

He sighs. "We were brothers, but it became different in college. Or maybe we just finally saw the truth of who he was. He'd been mistreated in foster care. Abused. Molested. Treated like garbage all around. All of us had been, but he probably had it the worst. No one could deny that. He'd always had a temper. I mean, who could blame him? He did weird stuff when he got mad—lashed out, said awful things, but...we knew why. We understood him, and we tried to be there for him like other people couldn't. No one understood what we'd gone through aside from us. Anyway, he started getting worse. Angrier, more cruel. Things started going south throughout most of our senior year of college, and then one night...he just flipped." His eyes are distant. Haunted. "I'd never seen him like that."

"Was it the night Aubrey Vance died?"

His eyes go wide as they flick up to meet mine. "You already know about her?"

"Vaguely, yes. I don't know what happened."

"No one does. No one but the five of us. Well, I guess the two of us now, if Tate's still…" He stops talking, looking down. "It was never meant to happen. Never. But we should've stopped it. Truth be told, we were scared of him. Not just physically, but…emotionally, socially, he could've destroyed us. We never thought he'd take it that far. Never. Please believe me. We had seen him do some messed up things, but we'd never seen him as awful as he was that night." He drops his face into his hands. "Or maybe we just never let ourselves see it. He was our brother. We wanted to believe he was good, that he'd become good, grow out of it. We wanted to see the best in him. We didn't think he'd actually…" He looks out the window, pressing his lips together. There's no denying the horror behind his eyes. Whatever he's remembering, it was terrible.

"He killed her? The professor?" My coffee roils in my stomach. I feel like I'm going to be sick.

Slowly, Aaron's dark eyes turn to meet mine. "Yes," he says. "Yes, he did."

CHAPTER TWENTY-NINE

TATUM

Highland University
Twelve Years Ago

I slam her head into the back of the chair, and searing pain shoots through me. I'm bleeding, but in the shadows, I can't see enough to tell how bad it is. I'm still hanging on, still attached at least, but it's bad. I'm dizzy from the pain. The sound around me is fading and fuzzy.

I'm going to pass out. I really think I'm going to pass out. I stumble backward in a vengeful fury. The boys just stand there, half of them with their hands covering their own dicks, like it's them who has been attacked, not me.

I turn back to her, seeing red. Nothing makes sense except the fact that I'm going to kill her. I can see nothing else. I grab hold of the chair she's in, using every bit of my strength to swing it around and to the ground. It cracks with the blow, and then light explodes. Bright white light everywhere. No. *Fire.* Fire is everywhere. Shit. *She's on fire.* She landed close to the in-ground firepit, but not in it. Not on it.

What is happening?

She rolls around, half her body still attached to the chair, flames engulfing her hair and skin and clothing.

The vodka. It was on her hair. Her clothes.

It was everywhere.

She's screaming, but I can hardly hear it. Like I'm underwater. My entire body trembles as I watch the scene unfold.

I stagger backward, watching in horror as the boys rush forward. We have no water, no way to put it out. Matteo takes off his letterman jacket and whips it over her, trying to suffocate the fire while the others shout instructions, telling her *to roll, to run, to stop moving, to hold still.* Matteo's jacket ignites with flames quickly, and in a panic, he drops it on top of her.

Her screams are animal-like, even as dulled and muted as they are to my own ears. No one is looking at me. No one sees the horror on my face. It wasn't supposed to go like this. It wasn't supposed to...

I was supposed to play god tonight. The fire took her before she had the chance to beg for her life. Before she had the chance to say she was sorry for her mistake. That she wanted me so badly she couldn't help herself, perhaps. Before the boys gave me the apology

I'm owed. I was supposed to be in charge tonight, and I lost that chance.

My body is strangely numb, like I'm not really here. Like this is all a dream. A nightmare. My worst nightmare.

It takes far too long, but it is over far too quickly. Her body is still burning, but her screams have stopped. The air is filled with the scent of charred flesh, like an unintentional barbecue.

When they look at me, I fix my face. I can't show them this wasn't intentional. I can still salvage this if I make it look like this was my plan all along. If I let it, this can be my most valuable lesson ever.

I step forward, owning my power, shutting out the pain I feel, the blood that's dripping down my legs, and breathing in the scent of her searing flesh as if it's my favorite smell in the world. I point down at her, my body numb at the waist, my muscles shaking like I've had a long workout. I can't let them know it, can't let them see it. They can't see my weakness.

"Do. Not. Fuck. With. Me." Each word is its own sentence, each syllable spoken through gritted teeth. "Have I made myself crystal clear?"

The boys stare at me in outright horror, most of their bodies black with soot and ash from trying and failing to save her. Matteo's hands and arms have fresh blisters across them.

"Good. Now, then, let's get the fire put out and find somewhere to bury her." I turn my back to them, kicking her hideous bag out of my way. A book goes flying out of it and into the dirt: *The Catcher in the Rye*.

Stupid little bookworm.

I need to sit down, or my legs are going to give out. My vision has started to blur, and I'm afraid I'm going to lose consciousness. I move back to my bag to find something to wipe myself off with and assess the damage she did. I drop to the ground and squeeze my eyes shut, one hand on my head as a sound rings in my ears. I can't breathe. My chest is tight.

I reach into my bag, looking for something, anything. By the time I realize the ringing in my ears is the sound of him screaming, it's too late.

I turn back just in time to see Matteo charging at me, the empty vodka bottle held in his hand. I spin toward him a second too late, a second too slow thanks to my sluggishness, and the bottle connects with my head. I feel it shatter, feel my head hit the ground.

Then it all goes dark.

CHAPTER THIRTY

CELINE

I listen in horror as Aaron paints a picture for me of the night everything went wrong. It's a picture straight out of a Stephen King novel—burning flesh and a dying girl, a boys' club of men too scared to stop their monstrous leader.

Except in this case, their monstrous leader is the man I love. The things he's telling me about what happened that night, about what Tate did, it doesn't sound possible. There is no way I've spent the last nearly twelve years looking into the eyes of a man who was capable of this.

"And so, he killed him. Hit him with the bottle, and when it broke, he used that to slash his neck. He didn't plan to do it, it was just...it was pure instinct. I saw it on his face. And I think we were all glad it was done, even if it killed us just the same. I guess in a way, it took everything that happened for us to realize Tatum was never going to stop, no matter how much we wanted him to."

I jerk my head back, this part of the story not making sense. "Wait, Matteo killed Tate?"

His eyes drill into mine, dancing back and forth, like I should be catching onto something I'm clearly not. "No. Matteo killed Tat*um*."

"I don't understand."

His smile is small and sad. "Celine, the man you married is not Tatum Thompson."

My body goes cold as the wave of information washes through me. "What are you talking about? Of course he is."

"Tatum hated nicknames. He made us all go by our full names, said nicknames were for lazy people and little girls. I think most of us called his mom Mrs. T just to mess with him."

"So, what? That doesn't mean anything. He changed his mind. Grew up. That night…it changed him. He's told me so himself."

"No. You're not hearing me. Tatum Thompson died that night in the clearing off campus. I watched it happen. I…" He stares down at his own hands as if they're covered in blood. "I buried his body."

"I don't understand." I pinch the bridge of my nose, squeezing my eyes shut. "If I didn't marry Tatum Thomspon, if Tatum Thompson is dead, what exactly are you telling me?" I refuse to believe it. I can't. It's impossible. I'm not convinced this man isn't delusional at this point. That this isn't all some cruel prank.

"The man you married is—*was*—Matteo Acri," he says, and my breathing stops, my chest suddenly hollow as if someone has scraped the contents out with a spoon. I open my mouth to say something, anything, but he's not done. "Or, as he always liked us to call him when Tatum wasn't around, Tate."

I feel like someone has reached into my chest and driven a screwdriver into my lungs. *It's not possible. It's not possible. This can't be true. He's lying, but why?* "That's impossible. I've seen his driver's license. I married him, for goodness' sake. I saw his birth certificate. I'm not an idiot."

"A birth certificate that listed parents you know aren't his birth parents." His smile is twisted, like he feels conflicted.

"So?"

"So things aren't what they seem already. You believe the reality you were handed, the story you were sold."

"I believe I married Tatum Thompson." I drop my hands, finding a flaw in this story. "Hang on. You're telling me they switched places, and what? His parents didn't notice? I have a picture of the five of you. Matteo and Tatum might've looked similar—they were around the same height, pale complexions, and brown hair—but they weren't twins. There's no way Matteo could've fooled people into believing he was Tatum. Certainly not Tatum's own parents."

His head bows with a slow, contemplative nod. "The Thompsons are good people. They treated us like sons. They were parents to us when we'd never had any parents. When they adopted Tatum, I think we all breathed a sigh of relief. We had somewhere safe to go when our foster parents didn't care where we were. When they'd rather us not be with them." He rubs a hand over the side of his face. "To be honest, I always wondered if Tatum was the reason they didn't just adopt all of us, if he put a stop to it somehow. I always sort of assumed he told them not to after they'd met us, but I'll never know that for sure." He sighs, his face seeming to age almost right before my eyes. "After we buried Tatum, Matteo wanted us to leave Aubrey's body where someone would find her. He wanted her family to have answers, to get to say goodbye. To honor her. None of us were in our right minds at that point. We were preparing to go to jail, for our lives to be over for what we'd done. And so, we went to the only safe place we'd ever known."

I piece it together before he says it. "The Thompsons' house?"

He nods. "It sounds crazy, I know, but they were the closest thing we had to a family. We'd known them almost as long as they'd known Tatum, and we'd been there for every holiday, every school break since tenth grade. Daphne was the one who made sure we'd been to the dentist and forced us to go to the doctor when we were sick. So, even if she couldn't forgive us for what we'd done, we all felt we owed her the truth. And that's what we gave her. The whole truth. Every horrible detail. We didn't make ourselves look any better. We were monsters, too. We stood there. We watched as he did what he did. We allowed him to do what he did. Not only that night but for years. We enabled him and made excuses for him and laughed along with him, until the moment it all went wrong. We allowed him to become who he was. And I guess I want to say it's because we knew why he was that way. We'd seen all the hell he'd been through. We also felt loyalty to him that I can't explain. We wanted to believe he could and would change. But it doesn't matter. There's no excuse for it."

He drops his head, looking at the tabletop. "And when it was all over, we told her we'd show her where his body was if she wanted us to. We told her we were going to turn ourselves in to the police, but before the media could spin the story, we wanted her to hear the truth straight from us."

He has tears in his eyes when he looks back up. "But instead of turning us away, instead of calling us monsters for killing her son, she just cried. She just cried, and she held us, and...I still don't know why she did it. We weren't hers to protect. Tatum was."

I swallow, unable to speak.

"Matteo was the one who'd done it. He was the one

who needed her the most, I think. He'd lost the woman he loved. He'd killed our brother. And then Daphne said something I'll never forget. She took our hands and pulled us in close and said, 'We're going to fix this. No one is going to miss Matteo Acri. No one is going to report him missing unless we do.'"

I flinch at the harsh words.

"I know," he says, not missing my reaction. "But she was right. By that point, we were all out of foster care. Legal adults. We lived together in the dorms. We all interned at Mr. T's company. There was no one to miss any of us. If she reported that Tatum had gone missing, there would be a big police investigation. He was the son of a media mogul, and whether or not he was liked, he was well known on campus. But if Matteo Acri went missing? If any of the rest of us went missing?" He scoffs. "I think there was maybe one article written about it. No news reports. No one ever even reached out to me for an interview. No one cared."

"They really switched places? You're serious?" It's not possible, but it's true. It feels like my life motto these days. My mouth is dry as I wait for him to confirm what he already has. I don't want to believe it, but I can see the truth of it in his eyes, hear it in his words. My marriage, my life, my entire world, has been a lie.

He nods.

"And Lane just went along with it? Their entire family?" As I say it, I realize the truth: the Thompsons have no family. Employees, acquaintances, friends, sure, but no parents, no siblings. It was always just them and Tate. For as long as I've known them, and apparently even longer.

"I don't know what discussions went on behind closed doors to get Mr. T on board, but like I said, we all worked for him. We were close. I think—I hope—he thought of us like sons as much as we thought of him like a father."

My hands are like ice, so I tuck them under my thighs, thinking. Not only was I lied to by my husband, but also by my in-laws. Lane and Daphne have known all along that Tate isn't Tate. They've lived for years with this secret, protecting him and the rest of the boys. How can they do it? How can they call him the wrong name? The name of the son they lost? How could they just let him be buried and forgotten about?

"I can't believe this. I can't believe any of this. It seems impossible." Aside from my parents, Tate, and the boys, Daphne and Lane are the closest people in my life. I would do anything for them, but this? They've lied to me every single day with smiles on their faces. They lied when I asked about Matteo. When I showed them the photograph. They always knew who he was, and that he was the man I married to boot. The boy I was pointing to in the photograph was Tatum. The boy they claimed not to know was their own son. It's all too much to take in.

How can I ever trust them again?

How can I ever trust myself?

I let liars into my house. Into my world.

I let them around my children.

"They had Matteo drop out of college right away—as Tatum, of course. Needless to say, he wasn't missed. We reported Matteo as missing, but again, no one really searched for him. They found Aubrey a few days later, and that became a bigger story, which totally drowned out Matteo's disappearance more than it already was. The Thompsons moved a few hours away. Like you said, Matteo and Tatum looked similar enough for Matteo to eventually renew his driver's license as Tatum. Tate." He shakes his head. "It shouldn't have worked. I think we all just kept waiting for the rug to get pulled out from under us, but it didn't."

"Until now."

He nods. "Bradley fell in love, and he wanted to tell his fiancée the truth. I called Tate to tell him he should warn Daphne, to ask her what we should do, but before I got an answer, Tate was gone and Bradley and Dakota were dead."

"So you think the fiancée is doing this?"

"No. I really don't know what to think. At first I thought so, but now I'm worried…" He pauses.

"Worried what?"

"Tate came to see me a few days before he disappeared. He kept telling me how if anything went wrong, his life would be ruined. *His* life. He had the most to lose from all of this coming out."

I swallow, realizing what he's implying. Suddenly, my anger at Tate dissipates, and I feel only the need to protect him. To defend him. "You can't think he'd do this. You can't think he'd hurt anyone. Not now."

"I already told you what he's capable of when he's cornered. He killed Tatum when his back was turned. In cold blood. I'm not saying he didn't deserve it because we all wish we'd been brave enough to do the same, but just...be careful, okay? Now you know everything. Do with it what you will." He holds his hands up, finally grabbing his sandwich and taking a bite.

As he chews, I look out the window, processing all I've been told. My head is dizzy with the truth of it all, the lies of it all. Nothing about my life is what it seems. I've been lied to for years about the most fundamental things. My husband is not who he says he is.

Does that matter? At the end of the day, what matters most? His name or the person I know him to be? The human I know him to be? Can someone fake kindness and love? Could he have been pretending all this time? I know the light behind his eyes. I know the way he cried when he held each of our boys for the first time. The way he chased after them when they learned to ride bikes. I know the man my husband is, but I've been lied to so many times, how can I ever trust him again?

My circle that was already so small feels smaller now, laden with liars. Foxes in the henhouse. Mice in my house.

Nothing is what it seems, and I'm the one who has to deal with it. I have to tell Tate what I know, but only if it's safe. If Aaron is right, if I'm misjudging Tate again, trusting him when I shouldn't, I could be putting myself in danger by meeting him tonight, even more so if I tell him what I've learned.

I'm walking a thin line, and the only person I can trust right now is myself. Problem is, I've trusted myself all along, and I've been wrong.

What am I going to do with that?

CHAPTER THIRTY-ONE

CELINE

That night, the boys are at my parents' house, safe and sound, and I'm pacing the floor of the living room, trying to decide if I've just made the worst decision of my life.

I contemplated telling my parents everything, but I didn't. I still don't know why. Maybe because I didn't think they'd believe me. Maybe I thought they'd believe I was having a mental breakdown and needed the boys taken away. Or maybe...just maybe, I still want to protect him.

Does that make me a monster or a fool? Even knowing all he's done, I also know the man he's been to me. That man isn't capable of hurting anyone. Not anymore. Maybe that makes me the most gullible fool in the world.

When I spot a pair of headlights driving down the road of our subdivision, my heart races in my chest.

There are knives in the kitchen. Lamps all around. A few of the boys' soccer and T-ball trophies. Heavy objects, but could I use them if I needed to? Would I be willing to hurt him if it came down to it?

A truck pulls into the driveway, and my brain begins to short-circuit as panic races through me. *Why did I agree to this? Why didn't I tell anyone my plan? Why was I so, so stupid?*

I think back over the expressions on my in-laws' faces as they looked at the photo I'd shown them. Their sons. Their sons that they loved and protected. Perhaps now their son is coming to protect them, and more importantly, their secret...from me.

But I would never tell. He has to know that. I would keep his secret with everything in me. I always would have. He only killed because he had to. He took a monster out of this world. I couldn't hate him for that. I can only sympathize with him and wish he'd trusted me enough to tell me the truth years ago.

A dark figure walks across the porch, and I recognize the shape of his body. It's the same one that has slipped across our bedroom in the dark after locking the door. The same one that has held me when I cried or when I was sick. The same one I've leaned on or snuggled up next to so many times over the last decade.

When his face comes into view in the porch light, tears blur my vision. *He's here. He's real. He's alive.*

I pull the door open and step back. "Tate..."

I don't know whether to tell him what I know or

keep it in—whether being honest will put me in more danger or if I can reassure him that I will protect his secret with my life, that all is forgiven. That I love him enough to look past all of this.

His eyes are stony and distant as he stares at me. "Are the boys…"

"At my parents'."

He shuts the door behind him, keeping his distance from me when all I want to do is hold him. "No one else is here?"

The question douses my skin with ice water as I remember Aaron's warning. My eyes flick toward the door, and I can't help thinking about the fact that he's blocking the exit. "No. Just us." *Idiot. Idiot. Idiot.*

He clasps his hands in front of him. "I have so much to explain and probably not a lot of time."

I nod. "I know."

He puffs a breath of air through his nose. "I'm sorry about all of this, Celine. I'm sorry I disappeared. I'm sorry about the money. I'm sorry if I ever put you in danger."

"Tell me everything," I beg. "I'm here to listen and to help you. I love you."

We're feet apart, and all I want to do is run to him and hug him, to know that we can get through this no matter what, but I can't move. I don't. I need to understand first.

He looks down, pacing listlessly. "The first thing you should know is that I'm not…my name isn't…"

"I know." I don't mean to say it, but I need to have it out there. He's struggling. He's scared. I can see it in his eyes. I need him to know I'm not running away.

His eyes go wide. "You do?"

"I know your name is Matteo."

Tears flood his cold eyes, and he blinks them away, looking out of the room. "I didn't lie to you when we met. When I told you my name is Tate. There have been so many lies over the years, but that wasn't one of them. My parents used to call me Tate, before they…" He sniffles. "My real parents, my birth parents, died when I was six. A drunk driver ran a stoplight, and just like that, they were gone. I don't remember much about them, but I remember that they called me Tate. I didn't lie to you when we met. Even though I couldn't tell you the truth, I tried not to lie."

I nod, chewing my lip. "I know. I know why you did what you did. I know what happened the night the real Tatum died."

He opens his mouth, trying to say something, but tears choke out his words. "When I got put into foster care, Tatum was there. And Dakota. And Aaron and Bradley. We were brothers. They moved us from home to home, and sometimes I was alone and sometimes one or two of them were there, but the best homes… the best ones were when it was all of us." He pauses, composing himself by swiping his hand over his face. "I loved him. Despite everything he did, despite the monster they made him into, I loved him, Celine. What

I did that night…I wasn't myself. I was so angry with him, and I just wanted it to stop. I knew it wouldn't stop. It doesn't make it okay. It doesn't make me any better than him."

I can't stop myself. I step forward, trying to hug him, but he puts his hands up, stopping me from getting any closer.

"I need to finish telling you the rest," he says.

"Okay." Feeling a bit like a scolded child, I step back.

"We lost touch after everything. Dakota tried. He wanted to get us back together, but…I couldn't. I couldn't look at them and see the way they looked at me. I took him away from them, too. I killed their brother, too." His voice cracks. "I'll never understand why Daphne and Lane helped me, why they protected me, but I'll forever be thankful because it meant I got you. And the boys. And you guys are the best thing that has ever happened to me."

Tears pour down my cheeks at his words. Why does this feel like goodbye? Why is he saying it like this is over? Like he's still planning to leave?

"And so when Aaron called me and told me Bradley was going to tell his fiancée the truth, and then I eventually heard from Bradley about it too, I went to Mom in a panic. She'd always made things better. I wasn't afraid of the truth coming out. I wasn't afraid of going to jail. I was…I was afraid of losing you. I was afraid that you'd hate me. That you'd see me as a monster."

My heart aches for him, for this truth that he's kept

buried for so long. For there being so much he had to keep hidden from me. "I know why you did it. Tatum was the monster. Aaron told me everything."

He shakes his head. "No. We shouldn't have let it happen. We should've told the truth back then and taken the consequences. Then your life wouldn't be messed up, too. Then you wouldn't be in the middle of this."

"The middle of what? Whatever happens, we can face it together," I promise him. "I love you."

"Not this. I can't put you in the middle of this. I have to fix it somehow."

"Fix what?" I demand, staring at his face in the glow of the lamp. I don't understand.

He takes a deep breath, running a thumb over his opposite palm. "Mom promised me it would be okay. That she and Dad would handle it. And then...Bradley died."

My skin goes cold. "What are you saying?"

"And when I asked her about it, she said it was awful. She sounded genuinely upset. I wanted to believe she wasn't involved, that she could never hurt us, but...I don't know. And then Dakota told me he was being followed. That someone was trying to scare him by following him around, and that they'd left a burned book at his house. A burned copy of *The Catcher in the Rye*, which was the book Aubrey had in her bag that night, the book that we left with her body. No one would know about that except us. And my parents. I thought he was being paranoid at first, until...until I saw the car that was following him. And I recognized it."

I wait, silently begging him to go on as he pauses.

"It was my dad." He looks up at me, tears glimmering in his eyes. "My dad was following him, and I worried he was going to do to him what he'd done to Bradley. So, I took the money from our account to split it between the two brothers I had left. I was going to give it to Dakota and Aaron. To tell them to run, to beg them to go. To hide. And then, on the day we went to move the body, to protect our secret from even my parents, I traded vehicles with Dakota, thinking my dad would follow me and I could confront him. But he must've seen us trade places. I have no idea where he was, but the next thing I knew, Dakota had been run off the road, and I was hiding out in a hotel room trying to get to Aaron to warn him without getting caught."

"Your dad is the one doing this?"

He nods slowly. "And I don't know if he's trying to protect me...or himself."

"Perhaps I can give you an answer to that." I jerk my head around to see my in-laws standing in the hallway. In Lane's hand, he has a gun.

CHAPTER THIRTY-TWO

CELINE

Tate moves to stand in front of me, his hands behind his back to hold mine. I squeeze his hands, so grateful for the small piece of comfort, but it does no real good. I'm trembling as I stare at two of the people I've trusted most in the whole world, people I've trusted in my home and with my boys.

Without warning, Daphne rushes forward, throwing her arms around her son.

He hugs her back, his body stiff, as Lane lowers the gun.

"I don't understand," I say, stepping out from behind my husband.

"Your mom said you wanted her to have the boys tonight. We worried about you being here alone," Daphne says. "So we thought we'd drive by. And then when we saw the truck was here, we didn't know who it was. So we went around the back to make sure you were okay."

"You were protecting me?" I ask, my voice trembling. "You broke in to protect me?"

Looking sheepish, Lane says, "I had the back door key. I would've never used it if I wasn't worried you were in danger."

I look at my mother-in-law, whose eyes are full of fat tears. "Oh, sweetheart, of course we were protecting you." She squeezes me tight. "It's all we've ever wanted to do—protect our kids. I'm so sorry. About everything. I'm sorry you're in the middle of this."

"Protect your kids?" Tate says, his voice breaking as he pulls me out of her arms. "To protect one, you killed the others?"

"No," Lane says quickly.

"No," Daphne agrees.

Lane goes on, "Tate, we didn't. We wouldn't. You have to know that, son. I tried to talk some sense into them. I went to Bradley first, yes. After you told your mother what was going on, that he was going to tell someone about what happened that night, I went to him to try to protect not just you, but all of you. You're all my children." His eyes land on me. "All of you. And I would move heaven and earth to protect you."

"So you didn't kill him?" Tate's voice is stoic.

"He told me I could come over that night because his family was out of town, but when I left, I swear to you, he was alive and well. Whatever happened after that, it had nothing to do with you. It kills me knowing

I left, and he died. It kills me not knowing if I could've protected him, but I would've never hurt him."

"And Dakota? What about him? Was that a coincidence, too?"

My father-in-law rubs his forehead. "I will never forgive myself for that because, yes, I am the reason Dakota is dead. But I didn't kill him. I didn't do anything on purpose. I'd gone by your office to try to talk to you about everything while you were away from the house that day and I saw you leaving. At least, I thought it was you. I flashed my lights and tried to get you to pull over, but you sped up. I panicked, thinking something was wrong, and drove faster, and before I knew what was happening, you crossed lanes and over-corrected and ran off the road. I thought I'd killed you." His voice breaks, and he looks down. "I ran over, tried to pull you out, but it was him. He was already gone, son. There was nothing I could do. He was just gone."

"So you left him?"

Soft, silent tears descend his wrinkled cheeks. "I panicked. I went home. I'd lost two boys. Two sons in a matter of days. What was I supposed to do?"

Daphne speaks up then, crossing the room to hold her husband while she looks at her son. "All we've ever wanted is to keep you safe, Tate. We knew if the police found out what you'd done back then, we'd lose you. Once we'd talked to you, once you told me about Bradley's plan, I was frightened. I knew we couldn't let any of them talk to the police or change their minds about what we'd all agreed upon years ago, but we were going to offer them money. We were going to help them see reason. We'd never hurt them. We'd sooner confess to the murder ourselves. He was our child, after all." Daphne wraps her arm around her husband, her eyes teary. "You all were. We loved you equally. And when we thought you were gone, too, it killed us. It destroyed us. We called your phone so many times just to hear your voice."

"Were you the one calling me?" I ask them, remembering the strange calls I'd received. "Or was it always you?" I look at Tate.

"I called every day," Tate says. "I missed you. I wanted to hear your voice, but I was also trying to listen for my parents, to decide if they were here. I wanted to warn you about them, but I had to make sure you were safe."

"You know we'd never hurt you," Daphne cries, covering her mouth. "Please tell me you know that. You're our son. We love you. And Celine. And the boys."

Tate crumples like it's all he's been waiting to hear. "I'm so sorry. I'm so sorry for everything." I get the feeling he's apologizing for much more than this. For everything before this. For all the things that have weighed on him over the years.

"Oh, honey." Now Daphne and Lane are crying, too. They gather their son in their arms, hugging him. "It's going to be okay. It's all going to be okay."

He turns back to me, a question in his eyes that he can't speak, and I nod. I'm still here. We're going to be okay, too.

I wasn't wrong about this man. I wasn't wrong about how much he loves me. I know who he is, and that's the greatest feeling in the world. Despite all the mess and chaos that we'll undoubtedly have to deal with and process after this, we have each other. We love each other, and he's home.

Right now, that's all I can bring myself to care about, so I hug my family and soak in this moment. All the rest can wait.

CHAPTER THIRTY-THREE

DAPHNE

One Week Later

With Tate home, everything is back to normal. I've never seen the boys so happy. Having their dad back, everything is suddenly right in the world.

I, better than anyone else, understand how important family is. For years, Lane and I struggled to have children of our own, and when we became foster parents, our hearts were broken again and again when babies we loved and cared for and protected were taken away from us, given back to the very people who had hurt and neglected them, only for those same children to return to us years later, even more hurt and lost than before.

When we met Tatum, we were told he was a lost cause. A boy no one wanted growing into a man no one would know how to love. But I thought we did. I thought our love could save him. I thought, given enough time, we could fix him.

But we couldn't. I saw that, though by then, it was too late. In every way that mattered, he was ours. He was surrounded by good boys, boys who cared, boys who tried despite their flaws. I hoped they'd influence him, but instead, he manipulated them.

It killed me to watch it happen, but despite everything, I loved him. He was my son in every way that mattered, and I would've gone to the ends of the earth to protect him.

I'm ashamed to say it now, but the day we learned he was dead, my first feeling was that of relief. I had spent years waiting for the day we'd get a phone call telling us that he'd killed someone, or taken a gun into a classroom, or something equally horrific. I understand now that there was nothing we could've done to fix him. Therapy didn't work because he wouldn't go to it. Unconditional love only made him angrier.

He was who he was before he found us, and there was no way we could've fixed him. It's a hard truth, one I still struggle with, but it is *the* truth.

Which is why, when the boys came to me and told me what they'd done, asked for my help in going to the police, I told them no. I protected them because no one had ever protected them before. I loved them in a way only a mother can, and I was their mother.

I was their mother in the only way I could be, and had Tatum not forbidden the idea, had I not been afraid he might murder them in their beds if I did it anyway, I would've adopted them as soon as I met them.

There was nothing I could do to go back and fix that then, but I could protect them at that moment, and I did. Convincing Lane to go along with it wasn't easy, but he understood. He loves those boys as much as I always have, and he'd do anything to protect them, too.

So we lied. We switched their identities. We made it all up as we went along and protected them with everything we had, and by some miracle, it worked. I said goodbye to one son—the guilty one—and protected the others.

I won't say it was easy because it destroyed me, but it was necessary. Just as other things have been necessary. When Tate told me Bradley was going to tell, I knew it couldn't happen.

I sent Lane, who couldn't reason with him, and then I stepped in. I never planned to hurt him. It killed me. It still kills me. My nightmares will forever be tainted with the way he looked when I hit him with that rolling pin. Had I believed there was any chance I could convince him to change his mind, I would've, but he was a man in love. Therefore, he was a fool.

Lane doesn't know. He can't. No one can.

Just as no one can know that I was going after the others next. Not Aaron—I knew he was just as freaked out as Tate after talking to him—but Dakota needed to know there were consequences if he ever got any ideas like Bradley had. I wasn't going to harm him, of course. I had no reason to. I simply wanted to fire a warning shot.

Keep your mouth shut and protect us all. Because my baby has babies now, and I'll be damned if I'm going to lose the family I gave my blood and sweat and tears for over someone else's guilty conscience.

I am not a monster. I am a mother, but when our babies are threatened, I'm not entirely sure there's a difference.

While Tate and Celine tuck the boys into bed, I step out onto the porch to listen to the crickets chirping. It's so peaceful out here.

I did that.

If I hadn't acted, this family would be in shambles. I protected their peace, and I protected mine.

My phone chimes with an email, and I open it, reading through the message. It's an automated review request from my favorite bookstore. Normally, I'm happy to review and help the authors I adore, but this time, I think I'll keep my opinions to myself. I press the button to delete the email and am met with a pop-up.

Are you sure you want to delete:
Review Request: Thank you for purchase of
The Catcher in the Rye?

Oh yes. I'm absolutely sure.

As much as I hate that so many people were hurt in

all of this, I'm glad there are fewer people out there to tell Tate's secrets. *My* secrets now. Secrets that could hurt my boy and my girl and my grandchildren. My family.

Secrets that can never get out.

I click *yes* and delete the email. It can't hurt anything now anyway.

I'm a much better secret keeper than my son could ever hope to be, and I'll take this little secret of mine to the grave.

WOULD YOU RECOMMEND THE GUILTY ONE?

If you enjoyed this story, please consider leaving me a quick review. It doesn't have to be long—just a few words will do. Who knows? Your review might be the thing that encourages a future reader to take a chance on my work!
To leave a review, please visit:
kierstenmodglinauthor.com/theguiltyone

Let everyone know how much you loved
The Guilty One on Goodreads:
https://bit.ly/theguiltyone

STAY UP TO DATE ON EVERYTHING KMOD!

Thank you so much for reading this story. I'd love to invite you to sign up for my mailing list and text alerts so we can be sure you don't miss my next release.
Sign up for my mailing list here:
kierstenmodglinauthor.com/nlsignup

Sign up for my text alerts here:
kierstenmodglinauthor.com/textalerts

ACKNOWLEDGMENTS

When I started writing this story, the premise came to me first. I saw Celine at the police station so clearly. I saw the most devastating day of her life turning into the most confusing. But from there...I had no idea where I wanted to go. I toyed with several different twists and endings, trying to figure out what exactly Tate's secrets were and who the man in his car would end up being.

Typically, when I write my stories, I start with the twist. I know where I'm heading and get to have fun with how we'll arrive there. For that reason, this story felt different from all but a handful of my others. It was full of possibilities as I weaved my way through Celine's world, discovering new secrets, changing things, adding and removing characters, and being shocked myself at how the story turned out.

Most of my books ask the reader a question. In THE GUILTY ONE, that question (in my mind) is: How far will you go, how much will you forgive, and what will you overlook in order to protect the people you love?

This story, one that I was originally calling GOOD

BOYS, is without a doubt one of my darkest, but it felt like one that needed to be told. Standing up to enemies can be easy, but standing up to friends is often difficult. Still, sometimes it has to be done. With this story, I wanted to play around with the ideas of loyalty, fear, family, and how we determine what the right thing is.

Thank you for going on this journey with me and trusting me to get us through it safely.

As always, this story wouldn't have made it to your hands without the support, advice, belief, and encouragement of the following people:

To my husband and daughter—I love you both so much. Thank you for being here for the fun parts and the not-so-fun parts. Thank you for celebrating with me for the highs and loving me through the lows. I couldn't do any of this without you both and I'm so incredibly grateful to get to experience every moment of this beautiful life with you.

To my editor, Sarah West—thank you for believing in every story I hand you and for helping me turn it into something worth reading. I'm so thankful for your insights, advice, questions, and trust. I love our little team and couldn't imagine taking this journey without you here with me.

To the proofreading team at My Brother's Editor—thank you for being my final set of eyes and polishing each story until it shines!

To my loyal readers (AKA the #KMod Squad)—oh my goodness, what a dream come true you are! All my life,

I've wished for people to read my stories and these last eight years with you have been all I could've hoped for and more. Thank you for every purchase, every review, every email, every tag on social media, every shoutout, every book club, and every single thing you do for my stories and me. Thank you for believing in me, for recommending my stories to your friends and family, and for returning time and time again to go on another adventure together. It means the world to me. *You* mean the world to me. Here's to many more adventures to come!

To my book club/gang/besties—Sara, both Erins, Heather, Dee, and June—thank you for everything, ladies. I'm so grateful to have the world's best, most loyal, loving, thoughtful, hilarious, and supportive friend group. I don't know how I ever did this without you guys, but I'm glad I don't have to anymore. Life is better with our group and I'll never stop being amazed that we found each other. Love you bunches!

To my bestie, Emerald O'Brien—thank you for being my sounding board, my cheerleader, my Maya, my Michael, my Naomi, my sharer of the moon, and the keeper of all my secrets. I love you, friend.

To my agent, Carly, and my audiobook publishing team at Dreamscape—thank you for helping to get my stories into the hands of as many readers as possible!

Last but certainly not least, to you, dear reader—thank you for taking a chance on this story and supporting my art. I will never fail to be amazed that somehow, out of all the books that you could be reading, you picked this one up and went on this adventure with me. However you found this story, I'm so glad you did. Thank you for trusting me to tell it and for being my wish come true. All I've ever wanted is to tell stories and with a single purchase, you made that dream a reality. Thank you for being a reader, for choosing books over so many distractions, and for being here with me. As always, whether this was your first Kiersten Modglin book or your 46th, I hope this journey was everything you hoped for and nothing like you expected.

ABOUT THE AUTHOR

KIERSTEN MODGLIN is a #1 bestselling author of psychological thrillers. Her books have sold over 1.5 million copies and been translated into multiple languages. Kiersten is a member of International Thriller Writers, Novelists, Inc., and the Alliance of Independent Authors. She is a KDP Select All-Star and a recipient of *ThrillerFix*'s Best Psychological Thriller Award, *Suspense Magazine*'s Best Book of 2021 Award, a 2022 Silver Falchion for Best Suspense, and a 2022 Silver Falchion for Best Overall Book of 2021. Kiersten grew up in rural western Kentucky and later relocated to Nashville, Tennessee, where she now lives with her family. Kiersten's readers across the world lovingly refer to her as "KMod." A binge-watching expert, psychology fanatic, and *indoor* enthusiast, Kiersten enjoys rainy days spent with her favorite people and evenings with her nose in a book.

Sign up for Kiersten's newsletter here:
kierstenmodglinauthor.com/nlsignup

Sign up for text alerts from Kiersten here:
kierstenmodglinauthor.com/textalerts

kierstenmodglinauthor.com
www.facebook.com/kierstenmodglinauthor
www.facebook.com/groups/kmodsquad
www.threads.net/kierstenmodglinauthor
www.instagram.com/kierstenmodglinauthor
www.tiktok.com/@kierstenmodglinauthor
www.goodreads.com/kierstenmodglinauthor
www.bookbub.com/authors/kiersten-modglin

ALSO BY KIERSTEN MODGLIN

Widow Falls

Missing Daughter

The Reunion

Tell Me the Truth

The Dinner Guests

If You're Reading This...

A Quiet Retreat

The Family Secret

Don't Go Down There

Wait for Dark

You Can Trust Me

Hemlock

Do Not Open

You'll Never Know I'm Here

The Stranger

The Hollow

Bitter House

The Guilty One

ARRANGEMENT TRILOGY

The Arrangement (Book 1)

The Amendment (Book 2)

The Atonement (Book 3)

THE MESSES SERIES

The Cleaner (Book 1)

The Healer (Book 2)

The Liar (Book 3)

The Prisoner (Book 4)

<u>NOVELLAS</u>

The Long Route: A Lover's Landing Novella

The Stranger in the Woods: A Crimson Falls Novella